T0402331

POINTED HAND

J. MANOA

An Imprint of EPIC Press
EPICPRESS.COM

Pointed Hand
Werewolf Council: Book #5

Written by J. Manoa

Published by EPIC Press™
PO Box 398166
Minneapolis, MN 55439

Printed in the United States of America.

Cover design by Candice Keimig & Neil Klinepier
Images for cover art obtained from iStockPhoto.com
Edited by Ryan Hume

Library of Congress Cataloging-in-Publication Data
Names: Manoa, J., author.
Title: Pointed hand / by J. Manoa.
Description: Minneapolis, MN : EPIC Press, 2018. | Series: Werewolf council ; #5
Summary: Now cramped behind massive walls, Riley must deal with being surrounded by two groups who want nothing more than to find and punish her. Left to fend for herself, she learns the truth about the tragic events which shaped her.
Identifiers: LCCN 2016946217 | ISBN 9781680765021 (lib. bdg.) | ISBN 9781680765588 (ebook)
Subjects: LCSH: Werewolves—Fiction. | Young adult fiction.
Classification: DDC [Fic]—dc23
LC record available at http://lccn.loc.gov/2016946217

EPICPRESS.COM

For 12I1 and 12I2

PROLOGUE

THERE WAS A LOUD BARK.

"Bradley!" Amanda yelled at the brown and white beagle staring at the front door. A brown spaniel ran in circles around it. The beagle barked again. "Bradley!" she yelled, covering the ears of the baby in her arms.

" . . . as Juneau saw a high of forty-eight degrees, beating the record set only a few years ago. Last week—"

A series of barks.

"Bradley!" Both dogs looked back at her, heads cocked as though they didn't understand why she was yelling.

" . . . temperature ever recorded in February, and it looks like we're about to pass that record once again."

"Better heat than cold," Amanda mumbled at the television. She paced over the living room carpet, bouncing the baby gently in her arms. Bradley, the beagle, scratched the base of the door. The spaniel, Eddie, stared up at the window. "Being stuck inside all day gets old fast."

"What was that?" Amanda's husband Michael said, leaning over the island in the kitchen on the other side of the first floor of their house.

"Nothing," she replied. "Just talking to the television."

"All right," Michael said, as he returned to the bubbling pots on the stovetop, "just let me know if it starts talking back. Then we might have to—" More barks and scratches at the door.

"Bradley!"

The beagle tilted his head, turned his ears toward her, then went back to staring at the door.

" . . . reports of continued unrest in Santa Faustina,

now known as Wolfland, New Mexico, where soldiers have taken to hourly patrols through the town after violence began over the new protection policy of every settle—"

A higher pitched bark.

"Bradley," Amanda said as an afterthought while stepping around the couch, cradling the baby's head as she sat.

" . . . own settlement has gone quiet following an attack by an unidentified anti-Wolf vigilante group that helped prompt the current policy of permanent protective custo—"

"Okay," Michael called out from behind the couch. "Dinner's—"

Amanda shushed him loudly.

"Jeez, just thought you'd like to—"

She shushed him again.

" . . . within the surrounding neighborhoods throughout the country," said the reporter. "Coming up, new studies find that a common household cleaner could be carcinogenic. More on that right after the break." A smiling family appeared in the reporter's place.

"Can I speak now, or are you really interested in the commercials?"

Another bark.

"Bradley," Michael scolded in a low tone. He stared at the dogs while Amanda walked the baby to the dinner table in the center of the room. There was that higher pitched bark again.

"See?" he said to the dog. "You're being a bad influence on your brother."

"It's like this every day," Amanda muttered, securing the high chair strap over the baby's blue overalls.

"People on the street," he replied, "enjoying the record highs."

"I hope you didn't make it too spicy this time." Amanda removed the lid from the large pot on the stove. "Gabby can't eat anything spicy."

"That's why Gabby has her own food."

"Is adding *less* pepper somehow *more* difficult?"

Amanda asked as she spooned rotini noodles onto a plate.

"It is if you like flavor."

"Hot isn't a flavor," said Amanda, carefully dipping the ladle into the sauce.

"Neither is bland."

Barks echoed from the front door in an arrhythmic mix of higher and higher tones.

"Bradley," Michael said calmly.

"I'm just asking that you make a dinner we can all enjoy." Amanda stirred a tiny bit of sauce among the noodles, "At least until—Bradley!" The barking didn't stop. "Bradley! Eddie!" The dogs scratched the door, barking incessantly. The baby shrieked before crying.

"Crap!"

"Hey, hey, hey!" Michael yelled as he stepped around the corner to the front door. "What's going on over here?" He was barely audible over the barking, the scratching, and the crying.

Amanda removed Gabby from the chair. She scooped

the baby into her arms, stroking her back to calm her as Gabby continued tearful screaming.

"It's okay," Amanda sang, "just stupid dogs." She leaned forward to see the door.

Michael was bent over to look through the blinds covering the front window. The beagle stood with his front paws on the door, nearly jumping with every bark. The spaniel darted in wide circles, barking, brushing both Bradley and Michael's legs.

"Dammit." Michael kicked Eddie away as he moved closer to the gap between slats over the window.

Amanda cupped Gabby's head to her chest, covering both her ears. "What's going on?"

"There's something out there."

"What do you—"

Michael fell back as the window shattered in front of him. He covered his face from the flying glass. Pictures crashed from the shelf under the window. Michael's hands twitched in front of him.

Amanda clutched her baby tightly, getting low to the ground. The blinds puffed out, holding in much of the glass, bending around the plastic trash can that had been launched. She strained to see through the gaps in the broken slats in the window cover.

The darkness seemed to move.

Michael checked the floor for glass before trying to stand. The dogs backed away, growling and barking like a warning. Amanda took a step forward, closer to the staircase to the upper floor. Gabby squirmed in her arms. The high-pitched wail quieted against the folds in Amanda's shirt.

"The hell was that?" Michael muttered as he rose up from the floor, carefully brushing glass splinters from his forearms. He kept one hand in front of him as he leaned toward the window again. "Amanda!" he screamed over the noise of the panicking animals. "Get Gabby up—"

Darkness shoved through the window. The blinds were ripped away in a wave. A wolf leapt into the window. Bright red eyes surveyed the room. Spit hung from an enormous jaw lined with spiked, crooked teeth. It seemed unreal—massive and hunched forward, stretching its neck out and curling its hands back, fingertips replaced with long razors, thick but sharp melted glass—like those hideous creatures she'd seen in blurry cell phone footage on television. She felt her knees trembling under her weight. News reports flashed through her mind, wild beasts that tore down walls and through defense forces assigned to hold them back. And now here was one of them, looking right at her, nothing holding it back. The wolf roared as it stepped into the house.

Bradley growled. Michael staggered back. He tripped over the spaniel circling his feet. Amanda felt herself freeze as the wolf's eyes locked on her. The creature seemed to smile. Bradley jumped for its heels. A massive arm swatted the dog across the room.

"Amanda!" Michael screamed again, "get Gabby outta—" The massive arm swung once more.

Amanda nearly fell over her own feet as she scrambled up the stairs. Her feet slammed the carpet in sloppy, panicked steps. She imagined the jaws snapping behind her, the claws swinging through the space she'd just left. She clutched the baby against her, using her other arm as though climbing a ladder to the upper floor of the house.

Get as far away as fast as possible.

She felt the baby's wail vibrating on the bones in her chest. She nearly slid across the carpet upstairs. She raced into the bedroom, flinging the door shut behind her. It slammed as though it would crack. The door wouldn't hold it back but could slow it down a little.

Get out of sight. Find a protected spot.

Bracing the baby, Amanda threw herself to the floor on the far side of the bed—his side. She pushed herself onto the floor, baby tight on top. Her neck pressed uncomfortably against the nightstand, forcing her chin down to her collar. Shafts of light shone through the blinds over the bedroom window above her.

"Shh, shh," she said in short breaths. One hand cradled the baby's back and neck as the other compulsively stroked the thin hairs covering her little head. Amanda felt her daughter's tears soaking through her shirt. "Shh," she said again, "shh, shh," as she reached to open the top drawer above her. She twisted to loop her hand into the drawer and groped inside, flicking her fingers blindly until she found it. The cold metal kept next to the bed. The just-in-case. She bounced slightly to wrap one finger just enough to pull it into her hand. She slowly closed the drawer. She clutched them both against her, baby in one hand, pistol in the other.

Gabby took a long breath. She let out a screaming cry.

"Shh," Amanda said once more, trying to bounce her daughter gently while straining to listen through her screams. "Shhhhh," she said. A loud footstep echoed on the staircase outside.

Another silencing breath preceded another cry.

Outside the bedroom door, the floor groaned. The door burst open.

There was a snorted growl from the doorway. Amanda tried to muffle the heaving sobs from her chest.

The creature was almost yellow in the streetlight coming in through the window, striped light and dark like a tiger. Even hunched forward, it still towered over her, barely fitting inside the room, its eyes glowing as though a fire raged behind them.

She held the baby's head tight against her with one arm, then closed her eyes and fired. There was a roar. She fired again. Another roar. She fired again. A vice clamped onto her wrist. It twisted. The bones snapped.

Amanda screamed. Gabby screamed. The creature growled, shaking the entire room. She opened her eyes to fire and jagged teeth. A series of snarled sounds rumbled from between its teeth, so low and broken and stretched that she could barely mark them as words.

"Quiet," the wolf seemed to say. "Pup."

Amanda's heart seemed to thump even more loudly than Gabby's cries.

A giant hand pressed over hers. The crying silenced under it. Blood dripped from the blade-like nails over each finger.

"You," she thought she heard, " . . . too long. Too . . . " It seemed to struggle with the sounds. " . . . too . . . comfortable."

On the floor, looking up, under the light, she saw only firing eyes and sharpened teeth.

"Taken too much."

She felt the pressure on her hand and chest. Pain flared in her wrist and through her arm.

"Not above the world." The wolf inched closer to her. It stank of dirt, grease, and blood. Hot breath broke across her face. "Not above nature."

She couldn't feel her fingertips.

"We are fury."

None of them.

"We fear you too long. Time for you to fear."

The pressure lessened on her chest. Feeling rushed into one of her hands. The other was still numb.

"Tell them," the wolf said, pulling away. The layers of light streaked over the short hairs on the side of its snout and the curved spikes of fur along its neck and shoulders. "Tell them all." It growled one last time before turning and walking away.

There was no crying.

Pain surged through the broken bones in her hand,

up her arm and into her neck. She felt the thin hair against her fingers. Her eyes drifted down.

No crying. No breathing. Tiny hands and feet lay limp. The little head rose and fell with Amanda's stuttered breaths.

Panic washed over her like a blanket smothering her, tightening until she'd suffocate.

There was no breath against her chest. There was . . .

There was a loud scream.

CHAPTER 1

"ALL RIGHT, WHO'S NEXT?"

Riley kept her head down as she stepped forward in the line. She peeked out from the edge of her hood to the person next to her, Shayera, who wore a long, fur-lined coat that looked as though it had been tailored to her slim frame. Riley's, on the other hand, had been salvaged from one of the abandoned apartments following the exodus from the town. The first exodus, the bigger one, when most of the regular humans like her left, and not the second, smaller exodus that followed the Pointed Hand's raid on the wolves who remained. The raid she'd helped carry out. Only fifty or so had escaped over the fence that night, but in a town of just over two hundred and fifty, that was a hefty percentage.

"Next," yelled a soldier at the front of the line.

The ruined elastic of her coat made Riley feel like a bell as she stepped forward another place in line. Strands of white stuffing peeked through a rip in the coat's shoulder. Still, the old coat and boy's jeans were less conspicuous than the thin, formless clothes she'd been left with after kicking her cloak across the museum floor. The scars on her face did enough to make her stand out.

" . . . about twenty miles from here," she heard one of the soldiers lining the fence say to another. "Killed the husband, the baby, even the dogs, but left the wife alive to tell the story."

An old man stepped away from the desk placed behind bulletproof glass and next to a metal door in what used to be the entrance to Riley's school. The crowd shifted slightly to let the man pass on the other side of the narrow corridor between high fences. His plastic jug sloshed in time with his steps.

"Damn animal," said one of the soldiers lining the fence.

"Next in line!"

Riley kept her head low but didn't turn as the old man passed. Looking away would be too suspicious, as would making eye contact.

"Sorry, Mrs. Willingham," said the female soldier sitting at the desk, "yer outta rations fer this month."

"But I—"

"You can get more on the first."

"What am I supposed to—"

"Next!"

"My husband is—"

"Next!" echoed a soldier hidden by the metal door with the slot that opened outward for deliveries.

The woman stood motionless for a moment.

"Please move so others can get through," said the woman at the desk. She had a noticeable mole on her round cheeks.

The woman glanced around. One of the soldiers lined up along the fence motioned for her to leave. The empty jug hung limp as the woman shuffled down the narrow passage across what had been the school's parking lot.

The fence turned to follow the road as one long, lonely passage up to the large wall that surrounded all those who'd stayed in the town, along with a few recent transplants discovered in neighboring cities. It wasn't a prison, though—the soldiers had emphasized that during construction of the black walls with the guard towers and floodlights that condensed the entire town into five square blocks between the two bridges—the residents simply couldn't leave the area, go out after dark, congregate in large groups, or approach the western gate, which the soldiers used for inspections during mandatory monthly supply drops. No, the walls were there to protect them from the outside world, like the group who'd infiltrated and burned their town less than three months before. With those walls, they'd never be able to do it again.

Only one person remained in line ahead of them.

Despite going through this exact entrance almost every day for three years, Riley felt entirely unfamiliar with it now. It was like looking in the mirror after taking Mr. Crawford's razor to her hair, or seeing her face after the bandages came off. She knew exactly what she was looking at but didn't recognize it. She knew it was the same place, or the same person, but . . . it wasn't. And what she had known, what she had grown accustomed to, it didn't exist anymore. It would never come back.

"Next!"

Riley remained a step behind and to the side of Shayera as she approached the desk pressed against the other side of the glass in the only school entrance that wasn't bricked.

"Name," the soldier said as she leaned toward the eight round holes drilled in the barrier. A horizontal slit just up from the top of the desk was the only other opening beside the steel door and the compartment for food deliveries. The door remained shut.

“Name?” asked the soldier wearing a desert camouflage hat. She still wore the body armor but without all the additional gear of the soldiers lining the fence: helmets with night vision, scoped machine guns, and, arrayed across the chest, a sheathed bayonet and four grenades, which resembled tiny garbage cans. She probably still had a weapon hidden behind that desk. Her own hidden blade.

Riley felt the pistol sagging in her interior jacket pocket. It was easier to conceal than the wrist blade, but seeing it wouldn’t immediately get her eviscerated by those living behind the wall. Not when there were millions of guns all over the country, not including the dozens held by the armed soldiers who surrounded the town every second of every day. Must be impossible to move in all that armor. Protective, but no speed or balance. No way to dodge except to take the hit and hope the armor was enough.

“Name?” the soldier asked again.

“Benally,” Shayera replied, “Gladys.”

Riley glanced up at this.

The soldier pointed to an inkpad and stack of paper inside the slit in the glass. Shayera rolled her right thumb through the ink and pressed it to a paper. She did the same for the left. It had to be the thumb, the theoretical divider between human and animal. Of course wolves, these wolves, had thumbs too. More like humans than any other species. The soldier took the paper as she flipped through a thick binder in front of her.

"Benally. Benally." She paused, looking up at Shayera. "What is that?"

"What's what?"

"Benally, where's that from?"

"My parents?"

"Where they from?"

"Here," Shayera replied, "or somewhere nearby."

"I guess you people got all kinds," the soldier said as she returned to the binder.

Shayera glanced back at Riley. Her dark eyes and features were still striking and sleek, even as a human.

"Says here ya get one more gallon and two rations and that's all fer the month."

Shayera replied with a nod, "I understand."

"Okay. One and two," the soldier behind the desk said to the invisible one behind the door.

The slot squeaked as it opened. Shayera placed her empty jug against the crook of the L-shaped cover. The soldier closed the slot to bring the jug in.

Riley kept her head low as she glanced around the edges of the fence, toward the two soldiers she'd heard talking earlier. They'd separated back to their stations again. The one closest to the school was tall and appeared wide in the shoulders, although that might have been the layers of armor. He had thick salt-and-pepper stubble and heavy lids that narrowed his eyes. Dark skin hung from them as symbols of fatigue, stress, or age. He caught Riley's pupils for a second before he looked away. Riley furrowed her brow at this. Why would he be the one to look away?

The slot groaned from the weight on the other

side. It squeaked as it pushed out. Riley put a hand out to keep the jug from rolling off the end.

"Okay, next!" yelled the soldier behind the glass.

Shayera grabbed the two packs of rations from Riley before passing her. Riley stayed close behind, head still lowered, hood still up. The remaining line shifted to let them pass. Riley caught up to Shayera once the line ended in the passage toward the road.

"Gladys?" Riley asked.

"Shut up."

"What? I didn't know Shayera wasn't your real name, is all."

Shayera was silent as they reached the turn toward the wall gate.

"And now I know why you changed it."

A grumbled response was lost under their rushed steps and the water sloshing in the jug held in Riley's arm.

The chain-link fences on either side of the passage resembled baseball field backstops, tall and angling inward at the top, except with razor wire laced between the two sides. Overlapping angles made a mess of the corners. The passage led from the school entrance to a mass of black metal not quite as tall as the fence, but much more solid, with two rolls of razor wire hanging from the top, one inside the wall and one outside. A sliding metal gate protruded an inch from the wall, two inches off the ground. It covered an opening tall and wide enough for one average-sized person to fit through at a time.

Beyond the fence, the wall's exterior was lined with poles that looked like they'd topple over from the array of heavy floodlights. Riley could just make out the speakers positioned under the lights. Platforms topped the towers that looked over the wall between the lights. There, armed guards kept themselves warm by walking around the pillars that held up a thin roof. Amazing how quickly the military could work at "isolating an area" when it really wanted to. They were much better at this task than the previous sloppy attempt at putting up a fence around the town. Sprawling town, unobtrusive fence:

failure. Cramped space, complete control: success. But still, this was protective custody. They were not prisoners. That's what they were told before the wall went up.

Riley could still remember the crack of Samantha's softball-sized fist against her cheekbone. It was amazing she hadn't broken anything. She was strong enough to do so, angry enough. She must have held something back.

Samantha had seemed so together in the plaza, taking command immediately, spreading the word for people to go back to their homes while the National Guard moved into the town, calmly warning Riley of the consequences for betraying the Order and then welcoming her to the apartment Samantha had shared with . . . him.

That's when Samantha broke.

She fell into the bedroom behind the couch that

had been in the living room of their house but was now far too big for the space. She slammed the door behind her and locked it. Riley sat down and tried to ignore the sobs, screams, whimpers, howls, muttered threats, and curses. At least Nate had a door there, so his mother would have something to hide behind.

Samantha stayed in that room for the entire day as trucks rumbled along the street outside and helicopters flew overhead, even as frantic knocks on the door and calls of her name made Riley duck into the other bedroom. Samantha finally emerged when half a dozen armored soldiers bashed the door in with a battering ram. Her face was gaunt, as though completely drained.

They were hustled out onto the curb with everyone else who lived in the building. Samantha held Riley to her side, partly for support, partly to keep her obscured. Outside, the soldier with the mole on her cheek informed them that they had one hour to gather everything they could carry and take it to a new location. Everything else had to stay behind.

To Riley, the room smelled like confined dog. His clothes were strewn on the floor from ripped boxes. Samantha stood among them, an excessively large robe covering her, before dropping into one of the piles and smothering her face in the green henley Riley had seen him wear so many times despite the faded spots on the sleeve and shoulder. Samantha pulled in other garments as though trying to bury herself.

"He's not in any of these," Riley said finally.

Samantha said nothing.

"We need to go," Riley added.

Samantha pressed her face into the armful of clothes beneath her. Riley looked over the bare mattress on the floor where the sheets swirled into the clothes pile.

"He was yours too," Samantha mumbled into the material.

Was.

"Not anymore," Riley replied, remembering the last time she'd spoken with him on the couch in front of his other room. "This moment already happened for me." Samantha's back curled over herself, rounding over the pile like a scared bug trying to burrow into the dirt. "We only have an hour," she said to Samantha as she stepped from the room.

"There's a coat in my room, brownish-red. Probably won't fit but looks warm. Warm enough."

Riley nodded even though Samantha wouldn't see it. "Thanks," she said so that at least Samantha would know. "Leave his stuff. Trust me, it won't do any good."

They were marched across Big Bridge into an area just north of the school. Barricades had been set up between the buildings within a five-by-five block grid. There were already portable spotlights hooked to what Riley assumed were generators hidden under tarps, their ends trapped by thick bolts driven into the asphalt. It took just over one week for the walls to go up, as though the planning and materials had been lined up months before.

Registration started two weeks after the residents

were moved into the wall, just long enough for most people to run out of whatever supplies they'd brought with them. Just long enough for them to become desperate. By then the idea of registering names and fingerprints was more than worth it for a steady supply of food and water every month. Riley stayed home while Samantha, Shayera, and the rest of those who remained in the city placed their names on the list. It was best not to have the name McKnight even whispered among a city of wolves. Each resident then received the same amount regardless of size, age, activity level, anything. One portion for one person. Or for Riley, Samantha, and Shayera, two portions for three.

The gate opened with a loud metal-on-metal scraping. Three of the four soldiers to Riley's left pulled at handles connected to the plate covering one of only two openings into the Habitation Zone, as Riley had heard it called. The fourth soldier on her left kept his rifle ready, watching Riley and Shayera, along with the four soldiers on the other side of the passage. Three small slats cut into the metal just outside of the gate, big enough for a human hand to fit through, or a gun barrel, or one of those trash can-shaped grenades.

"Stop!" yelled the fourth soldier. The scraping ended.

Shayera had to bend a little to fit into the opening. Riley easily passed under. She couldn't help trying to remember how tall he was, how much he would've had to duck to enter. He was tall enough that he could place his chin on her head if he wanted during their goodbye hugs. She always grumbled, but it made him laugh. It was kind of funny the first time. Had he grown at all since she last saw him . . . as *him*? The scraping resumed as soon as they were through. There was no click or slam in the end, just a sudden stop.

Shayera hugged the rations to her body as they

continued on. Riley looked back to see a pair of soldiers watching through the slits in the wall. She pushed the water jug higher on her chest.

The bare wooden doors and planks stuck to the buildings still grabbed Riley's attention, despite being in the town for over two months. Piles of gutted wires, pipes, and other materials filled in the gap between the structures they'd been removed from. The black metal wall stood in stark contrast to the faded and worn brick facades with snowflakes stuck in their nooks and cracks. It was like living in a child's diorama: small and contained, with a constant reminder that you could never leave.

The wall cut across the curve to Tanacross Avenue between the school and the bridge. A block outside of the barrier was the cinema where she'd spent many afternoons, evenings, and even a few mornings, slouched in a seat as close to geometric center as possible. It was probably a shell by now, an emptied, meaningless space wearing the costume of what she'd known. Further down the same block would be another shell from what felt like a lifetime ago, even from the day it appeared in a video seen all around the world. The last day she really knew him. Shayera halted.

Three wolves lingered on the corner ahead. The exaggerated width of their shoulders marked them as males. The sight alone no longer alarmed her. It was one thing she'd grown used to. It was almost welcomed. At least there would be no surprises. She'd even come to understand their speech, whether it was from familiarity, or their own opportunity to speak more while in that form, without using her heightened senses. Luckily, the shadows over her eyes would not immediately give her away. Seeing them in a group, however, all in this form, alarmed her.

The largest of the three crouched on his hind legs right at the corner of the curb. A white strip ran slightly off-center down his chin and to his chest. The one across from him appeared softer, covered in dark brown fur with a curl that resembled a poodle. The last had dark gray patches among the black that covered his body. The large one with the stripe pointed his snout toward the pair of women.

"You know them?" Riley asked quietly, turning her face away.

"Not sure. Don't usually *see* them."

Riley glanced back to the wall. Soldiers were visible as shadows watching through the slits in the wall. She turned back, head down, and walked on. Shayera followed.

The striped wolf rose. He raised his nose, sniffing the air.

"Lot of food," he said of the two rations in Shayera's arms. The other two stood as well. "A lot for only you."

"Females don't need much," said the patchy one.

"Wasting while others need," said the striped one as he started to move closer.

Shayera stepped in front of Riley. She pushed her shoulders back, chiseled chin sticking out, rations tight under her arm.

“Do you know who I am?” she asked in a steady tone.

The striped one snorted.

“I am a representative to the Council.”

He snarled. “Council is nothing.”

“Council put us here,” said the curly-haired wolf.

Patches lingered a few steps behind.

“I piss on the Council,” the striped one continued. Riley turned away from his gaze. The soldiers’ shadows remained behind the slits in the wall.

“Girl has a gun,” one of them said.

“We have others to take care of,” Shayera said, her voice wavering. “No reason to fight among our own kind.”

“She’s not,” said Patches. He pointed one long, blunt finger at Riley. “I smelled her that night. Blackrobes. Hiding among us again.”

“She . . . She’s one of us,” Shayera replied. “The Council has—”

“Failed,” snapped the striped one, jolting forward.

Riley shifted the water jug in her arms, reaching

over to lower the zipper of her coat, ready to pull her weapon if needed.

"Blackrobes came in before," said Patches. "Murdered us. And you help her."

"Traitor," the striped one growled.

"I-I'm . . . " Shayera stuttered, "I'm a not a traitor. I'm a member of the . . . There's no reason to—"

"If I were one of them," Riley said, "how would I even get in here?"

"With the others," Patches replied. "The new ones, the outsiders. Come in here. Wait to attack. Just like last time."

"But you said you knew my scent," Riley countered sarcastically. "How can I be new?"

"A spy, a traitor," the striped one snarled, "doesn't matter." His lip curled to reveal a chip that made his top right fang sharper. "We are the strongest. In here. Out there. We deserve more."

Shayera stepped up with surprising strength. "The Code forbids this."

"The Code?" patches mocked. "The only code here is nature."

"'W-we of the blood shall nev-never harm another of the blood,'" Shayera stuttered.

"Strongest wins," Patches replied.

"N-never."

Riley checked the buildings around them. The wooden boards covered most of the openings, but there was no way to tell who would be inside or what they could hear—or, more likely, smell. The striped wolf started to advance.

"Take our home," the striped one growled, eyes locking into Riley's, claws extending, "take our land. Should kill you. Here or out there. Kill all of you."

The other two followed behind. She reached for the pocket inside her jacket. She felt the grooves of the pistol grip against her fingertips.

A gunshot shattered the air. It echoed down the street.

"Disperse!" yelled a soldier behind a slit in the

wall. A pair of rifles lowered into position. "Disperse or we will fire!"

Riley placed her hands in the air. Shayera put down the rations to do the same.

"You know the rules," yelled the soldier, "no more than four at a time."

The striped one snorted loudly, glowering at Riley and then at the wall behind her.

"Small place," he said, "no escape. We'll find you." He swung his heavy body around, walking away before dropping into an easy run and disappearing behind the building on the corner. The other two vanished behind him.

"Damn animals," muttered one of the soldiers. "Should let them wipe each other out."

Riley hoisted the water jug back into her arms.

"What were you going to do?" Shayera asked as she scooped up the rations. "Fight? Expose yourself as one of them so everyone here would know?"

Riley zipped her jacket and checked the hood over

her head before stepping away. The water sloshed in her arms.

"People here would kill you if they knew."

"Secrets got us in here," Riley replied.

"That's freaking dumb," Shayera said, catching up.

Their steps were quick down the road. Footprints tracked them along the way. Their scent would as well. Riley secured the water jug in both her arms.

"Wolves hunt me here. Order hunts me out there," Riley said as they rounded the opposite corner from the others. "Does it really make a difference?"

CHAPTER 2

"HE WAS GATHERING SNOW FOR WATER. That's all. And they shot him."

Riley heard the voice faintly through the closed door to the ruined drug store, which they'd turned into their home after the wall went up. She looked over the rest of the area, slowing as she approached. The streets were clear of activity. She leaned over to see around a pile of scrap stuck in the alley across the road from their place. A torn end of a plastic tarp was waving from a stack of the metal shelves buried under pipes and cracked brick. She matched Shayera's pace and continued on.

"Shot him right there. Right through the—"

The woman jumped as Shayera opened the front door. The man next to her squeezed his hand on the shoulder of her dark green coat. He rubbed her back as they both stared at Samantha, who stood with arms folded.

"Right in the head," she continued as Riley followed Shayera into the room. "The head."

Riley shut the door behind her. She stepped around the counter, which remained in front of glass-covered shelves housing the prescription-only stuff, which probably hadn't stayed very long during the first exodus. Not that the small store had much to choose from in the first place. It had been the kind of place used when convenience was most important. Kind of like it was for Samantha and Riley when fleeing from the previous apartment. Shayera insisted on staying with them a few days later, once Maier shut himself off.

"We told him not to go outside," the man said, his orange jacket marking him as a sport hunter. "But he wanted to help. Our place is the last on the block before the west gate and . . . " his voice faded.

"Our son was a good boy," the woman added.

Shayera deposited the rations on the center of the counter. Riley passed her, placing the water jug on the far end. Shattered glass had been pushed into the corner of the room. Broken wiring still hung from the ceiling in places, the light bulbs long since torn from their sockets. Some of the pieces were probably in the corner.

"Never wanted to hurt anyone. Just wanted to help."

Samantha held her elbows in her hands.

"And they shot him just for getting near their gate. Just near it."

Samantha shook her lowered head. A long silence passed before she spoke.

"I'm sorry for your loss."

The couple stood there, quiet, as though waiting for more.

Samantha stared at the floor, her head bobbing weakly.

"That's it?" the woman asked. "*Sorry*?"

Samantha's body seemed to sink on each exhale.

"They murder our son and all you can say is sorry?"

"Becca," the man said, stroking the woman's back.

"You of all people should know what that feels like."

Samantha's gaze snapped up. Her face went blank and hard as stone.

"How old was your son when he died?" the woman continued.

"Becca."

"Seventeen? Kenny was fourteen. Fourteen! And they killed him. He was lying in the snow right outside of our door. We heard the shot!"

"I'm sorry," Samantha repeated, the stony

expression remaining. "My thoughts are with you and your son in this time."

"Thoughts? Oh thanks," the woman, Becca, said, tossing her hands up in faux celebration. "You can think about us. You can pray for us. But then you do nothing."

"Rebecca," the man said louder, removing his hand from her back and leaning in as though trying to get her attention.

Shayera turned away to stare at the brown ration containers. She bent forward as though reading the list of contents.

"They killed our son—our fourteen-year-old son—while he was collecting water for our family"—the venom built in her words—"and you do nothing. Nothing. All the time. Nothing. This happens over and over again."

"Honey," the man muttered.

"Kenny today, someone else next week, and more and more, and we do nothing. They kill us because we let them. Because the people who are supposed to act do nothing!"

Samantha's blank expression grew into one of strain, as though holding her words in was painful.

"High Councilor," the man said, "if you could please—"

"Don't call me that," Samantha snapped.

"We should have left when we had the chance." The woman said it like a threat. "Show the humans what it's like to live in fear."

"Mrs. Wallace, there's nowhere else we can go," said the man.

"Nothing but cowards in this town," Becca said. "At least out there we're fighting back."

Samantha's jaw clenched. Riley could see her nearly shaking with contained rage.

"Samantha," the man said, "please. You're the only one who can help. You of all people should—"

"Should what?" Samantha shouted, her facade finally cracking. "Relate to you? Being in some idiotic rebellion against the guards like you've heard about? You really believe that will lead to anything other than even more of us dying?"

"He was fourteen!" the woman shouted.

"Old enough to know not to go outside after the lights came on! Old enough to know that this is not a friendly place where he can do what he wants! This is a war zone! I've seen it." Riley noticed the moisture gathering in Samantha's eyes. "I know it."

"How can you say this to us now?" the woman snarled, not the feral snarl of a wolf, but the brutal one of a woman who'd lost a piece of herself.

Samantha straightened up. "Your son is dead," she said as one tear rolled down her reclaimed stony face. "I know exactly how you feel." Another tear formed. "I know every torment you're suffering right now. I also know what you do now."

The couple were silent, watching.

"You live with it."

"High Council, Mrs. Wallace. Maybe, if you please, just talk with the soldiers." The man twisted toward Riley and Shayera, whose back remained turned on all of them. “Or have one of the others do it for you.”

“There are no others, Mr. McCarthy. There’s only us. If you want to keep the rest of your family safe, then keep them close. Never let them get away from you.”

Becca was silent. Her husband was as well. Their shoulders sagged and heads hung in an asymmetrical parallel.

“I’m sorry for your loss.”

The woman’s head rose. “Coward.”

“If you would please,” Samantha replied, gesturing toward the door.

“What do we have to lose before we decide *no more*?” The woman asked as she stepped back, her husband already sulking his way around her.

“That’s the thing about loss,” Samantha answered, “eventually there’s nothing left.”

“Pathetic,” the woman spat. The man stepped out, but she remained, shaking her head, staring at Samantha, who stared right back. Samantha was a blank. The woman turned away. The wooden plank of the door shut quietly.

Samantha sighed.

Shayera muttered something so quietly even Riley couldn't understand it.

"If you have something to say, Shayera, you can say it to me instead of the wall."

Shayera stared at the rations in front of her, shaking her head.

"There's nothing I can do," Samantha said, turning her focus to Riley. "Even if I wanted to, there's . . . there's nothing I can do. Not anymore."

Another mutter from farther down the counter. Shayera stood there, eyes closed, head shaking, whispering as though in prayer.

"I heard it last night," Riley said, "the gunfire in the direction of the wall on that side."

"I can't stop the soldiers. None of us can."

Shayera mumbled to herself.

"It's not like they'd have any reason to lis—"

"You could at least try." Shayera finally turned

from the brown ration bags on the counter. "You could at least do *something.*" She threw her arms out in frustration. "Instead of just sitting around this damn"—she looked around the room—"whatever it is, feeling sorry for yourself all day."

"Well, what am I supposed to—"

"Nathaniel wouldn't have sat for months feeling sorry for himself. I saw what he was like. You saw what he was like." Shayera's lip quivered. "He didn't run away or cower when everything around him seemed hopeless. He might not have always made the right choice, he might've lashed out at the wrong people, but he'd learn to accept his actions and move forward. Do something, anything, to at least *try* to make things better. Instead of doing nothing to cause more nothing."

Samantha stood completely still. "And where did that get him?" she asked, a distance in her voice.

Shayera's shoulders slumped. "I can't believe I ever admired you," she said.

"I guess that was your mistake."

Shayera took a stuttered breath. Her head rose and fell in disappointment, eyes and mouth turning down as though about to begin a slow cry. She curved into herself.

"I—" Samantha started, "I didn't mean—"

Shayera stormed to the back of the store, to the staircase that led over to the bathroom along the rear wall. Samantha called after her, but she didn't stop.

Samantha slouched against the counter. She slid down to the floor. She hugged her knees and ducked her head against her arms. She stayed that way.

Riley's eyes wandered to the floor beneath her. She wiggled the toes on her right foot. A hole opened in the canvas top. The skate shoes she'd found after abandoning the thick boots given to her by the Order were already too thin for the weather. A hole wouldn't help. She lifted her foot to check the bottom. The cracks had worn at the ball of her foot, where she'd always been taught to carry her weight. She switched feet. The sole had started to pull away from the other shoe, exposing the toes of socks where individual threads barely held together. Frostbite may not be a concern for her, but mobility still was.

Riley placed her feet solidly on the ground. She rolled her weight back and forth, tapped her toes and heels on the ground. The shoes held well enough, but the last thing she'd need was to lose her footing during a possible confrontation because her shoe ripped open or slid on some ice or otherwise messed up her jump or landing. This wasn't about not falling in front of the judges, it was about not falling in front of someone aiming to kill her. Still, not much chance of finding a new pair in what remained of the town.

"We had some trouble coming back," Riley said, after what felt like a long period of silence. "Pests trying to get our food. Shayera . . . it rattled her. Funny how she could be so fierce when it came to standing against Dove but so hesitant against anyone else."

"She's spent her whole life believing in one thing

only to have it taken away from her," Samantha said, peeking up from her place on the floor. "I'm sure you know what that's like." She retreated back into the cave of her back and shoulders. "But she's loyal. To her kind at least."

"The soldiers eventually fired a shot in the air to drive them away. The wolves I mean, the pests."

Samantha didn't move.

Riley continued, "They were spouting on about newcomers and wanting to kill all the humans. They called Shayera a traitor for being with me."

Samantha raised her head to look at where Riley stood a few feet from her side.

"Did they know you?"

"One of them said he did, but"—she shook her head—"you know how people talk in here. Anyone they don't personally know is a spy, or a blackrobe sleeper, or whatever they want to call it."

"Except that for you it's true."

Riley glanced down to see Samantha staring up at her. "I'm not that loyal."

"Yeah you are. Your loyalty just belonged to someone else before them."

Riley slid down to sit against the counter as well.

"Did they follow you here?"

Riley shrugged. "Didn't see anyone, but how would I know? Can't exactly blink and see everything like you guys can."

"You should probably stay here unless you absolutely have to go outside. Like when they do the inspections. But stay near me. There are still some people who remember . . . when I used to do things."

"You know I used to wonder about that sometimes," Riley said, her tone picking up, "why you were always at home, why you rarely left and never worked, things like that."

"Did you have any ideas?"

"For a while I thought it was to make sure nothing happened between me and him. Nothing, you know, inappropriate."

A smile cracked Samantha's lips. "I was curious

about that for a little while but figured you were too good of friends for that."

Riley nodded.

"Was that all you came up with?"

"Well, once I heard that you'd get sick every few weeks . . . " Riley glanced over to where Samantha sat still with her elbows around her knees and her eyebrows lifted. "That's what I heard," she continued, "that you'd be sick. So after that I assumed you had some kinda disability that made you stay at home all the time."

"You never thought to ask what it was?"

"I did, when I first heard back when we were kids, but he said he didn't know. After that, I figured it would be a bit of a sensitive subject, and if he, or you, wanted me to know about it, then he would've told me."

"He would have too."

"I know."

Samantha looked to the back of the room.

"He would have told you everything if he could."

"I know," Riley said, nodding. "I would have, too, if I could."

Samantha straightened her back against the counter. "You know, there was never even supposed to be such a position as High Councilor." She stretched her neck and arms out. "The actual document, the one that was in the museum, was modeled after the sample structure outlined in the Nobilitate Nobis itself." She swayed her shoulders. "Or that's what we all believe, at least, since none of us ever saw the real Accord. Not like it was reprinted everywhere."

Riley shrugged in agreement.

"The idea was to create a self-governing settlement run by consensus, in order to keep one particularly charismatic individual from deciding against the will of all others." She glanced to Riley. "The Order has no such recommendation."

"Not surprising," Riley replied.

"But that kind of power structure isn't in our nature. Something in us—the 'wolf' part I suppose—gives us a predilection toward individual leadership." She took a breath as though disapproving of what she was about to say. "Basically an alpha."

"Ulrich," Riley said, remembering the conversations they'd had after leaving the apartment.

"Most people assumed that Maier would be the next in line, but again there was never supposed to be a High Councilor, so there can't exactly be a 'next in line.'"

"But then why did you take over?"

"Because it was what I had to do." Samantha took a second to gather herself before continuing. "After Pat, my husband, died, the Council was scared and outraged. Some people wanted to start shutting off the town from any new people, unless we knew their heritage. They even wanted to push out those who weren't like us." She tilted her head toward Riley. "Even your family."

She licked her lips before continuing. "Others were vicious. They wanted to slaughter every known member of the Order in revenge. Again." She shrugged. "Even your family." Samantha shook her head. "I couldn't let that happen. Pat had spent so many years working with your father to maintain all we had built here. I couldn't let that fall apart. Even with . . . what happened to him. Letting it be undone would've taken the meaning from his life." She breathed in deeply, letting her eyes shut. She exhaled slowly.

"Then why did you leave?"

Samantha sat with her eyes shut long enough to make Riley lean over to see if she was asleep.

"Because of Nate," she said, eyes opening again. "Because I didn't want him to know about what we are, what he . . . was. I didn't want him to know anything. I wanted him to live in blissful ignorance, as though such a thing were possible." She stared into the distance, somewhere beyond the rear wall of the small shop. "Never meant for anything like this to happen. Never thought it could. Not again."

"Me neither," Riley said. She leaned against the

counter. Brown stains covered the ceiling tiles. It never made sense to her that somehow dirt would remain on the ceiling. "Guess I never really believed this stuff was real. At least, not until I first saw it. Before that it was just," her gaze drifted over the empty light sockets and over to the divisions between window boards that allowed light into the room, "a way to regain what I'd lost. It was . . . a connection. Something I could do to heal myself. And maybe, like, a way to remember my father. What he would've wanted for me."

"Yeah. I bet Virgil knew that too."

"I'm sure he did." Riley's gaze continued to the dust and dirt left on the floor. "So," she said, "if you became High Councilor because it was necessary before"—she looked over to Samantha—"why don't you do it now?"

Riley saw a look of disappointment on Samantha's face, but continued anyway. "Even if you can't do anything to actually help, at least they'll have the comfort of believing someone is in charge.

You said it yourself that wolves, Fenrei, whatever you want to call your people, gravitate toward individual leaders. Why not be the alpha they need?"

"You have no idea," Samantha said almost as a whisper. "I've given everything I have. My husband gave up everything he had, everything he could." She gave a look like she was ready to scream. "You think I don't know who I am among my people? How else would I have been able to move myself and my son, my only family, into our own place? The owner of the home gave it to me after my husband died." She put her hands out as though in bafflement. "I asked to stay there for a while just to get away, and he ended up signing it over to me, on the spot. Same with most of our food and clothes, everything. They called it tribute." She threw her hands up. "After a few years I don't think most of them even knew why they were doing it. It was just what they did. Like a mindless tradition that people have forgotten the purpose of."

"So they took care of you," Riley said, her brow furrowing, "and you do nothing?"

Samantha's eyes were hot coals as they snapped to Riley.

"I've done enough." Samantha's tone was firm and cold as steel. "And you of all people don't get to question me about that." She pushed back against the wall to stand up. "Not you," she continued, turning to look upon Riley from above. "Not the one who dragged him into this because of some imagined destiny. Not you."

Seated on the floor, Riley felt tiny as Samantha towered over her, fingers twitching at her sides.

"You might live here," Samantha said, "but that doesn't mean you're one of us. You've never had to live with constant fear of being tormented or murdered for who you are. Had to know that anywhere you go there could be someone there who'd hunt you down. That the people who claim they're there to protect you, to watch over you, are the same ones who kill you. You never had to live with that." Her whole body seemed to shake. "You'll never understand. So you don't get to judge me."

Samantha turned away. She paced across the floor to the stairs in the rear.

Riley's breath pushed out of her like the air of a pipe organ. She slumped over, burying her face against the legs folded in front of her. She stayed like that until her back started to ache and the light faded in the room.

She blinked quickly. The shadows disappeared. Only those over her eyes remained.

CHAPTER 3

THE BRASS SECTION BLARED THROUGH THE SPACE between the wooden planks over the windows. A slight delay in the PA speakers jumbled the opening notes of "America the Beautiful" into a slur of scratchy noise. The song lasted exactly forty-two seconds before the static dropped into silence like a wave. Then the lights hit all at once, blasting bright shafts through the gaps and cracks in the wooden covers and shining dusty lines across the floor.

Riley was the only one who'd noticed them during the night. They were so intense they brightened even the inside of her eyelids. At least sundown was coming later, the cold decreasing as the year progressed. Estimating when the sun would go down—and for how long—was the only reason she cared to know what day it was. Well, that, and knowing how much longer the three of them would have to stretch two shares of rations and water, and when she'd have to pack up the pistol and metal cuff before the inspection came through. Other than that, there wasn't much importance between it being Monday or Saturday. Not like there was anything to look forward to.

Shayera poked her long snout through one of the spaces between the three boards over the front window. She knelt down, one sleek, black leg poking through the opening of the robe made out of a child's bed sheets. The light made her recoil slightly, but not nearly as much as it would for Riley, or any other person for whom it would have been blinding rather than merely annoying. Shayera sniffed at the cold air pouring through the gaps.

“Some still there,” she said with the unmistakable rumbling slur that came when a wolf tried to speak while in their animalistic form.

“Always are,” Samantha replied from her area near the back on the second floor of the old drug store. “Pointless gesture,” she added dismissively. She licked the last bits of beef stroganoff from her lean fingers. The puffy jacket made her look as though she were made of half-deflated bike tires.

Shayera sighed sharply. She slunk away from the window and slumped next to her bedroll against the wall. Her few sets of clothes and her worn-out shoes were piled next to an unopened ration on the floor next to where she laid her head.

Samantha tossed the food package onto the floor in the center of the room where other torn plastic containers littered the ground. “You should have some,” she said to the air.

Shayera nearly disappeared into the dark.

“Riley,” Samantha said, looking with a sort of tired sympathy that had become standard in the last few days. “C’mon,” she added, motioning for Riley to approach.

“I’m fine,” Riley replied.

“For food maybe.” Samantha held her hand palm out in the air. “But you should have some.”

“Fine on that too.”

“How long has it been since your last sacrament?” Samantha pushed herself up from the floor. “Three weeks? A month?”

“It’s still good.”

Floorboards creaked as Samantha approached. “Good isn’t good enough. Especially not here.”

Riley looked toward where Shayera had curled up on her bedroll with her eyes closed, probably pretending to sleep so she wouldn’t have to talk to anyone. There’d been a lot of that in the last few days: not talking.

“C’mon,” Samantha said, “just a little bit to keep your strength up.”

Dust rose through the shafts of light crisscrossing the room like a thin mist. Riley leaned forward to see through the boards, squinting as the brightness hit her. Somewhere outside, beyond the floodlights illuminating the city and the walls which contained its residents, there would be the rim of an actual sunset. It always began here before moving southward across the rest of the land, meeting its opposite somewhere in the middle. It would probably be an hour or two before the darkness reached her own mother, depending on where she was. Most likely California, where her brother and his wife lived. There'd been word of two Wolflands being set up in the desert to relocate those people found in the major cities. There'd also been word that these moves made many people very unhappy, not only in California but all over, with everything from hunger strikes to protest songs to full-on riots and rebellions exploding everywhere. She hoped her mother was far away from any of that. She never asked to be a part of this business. Werewolves, the Order, or what had been the Order—she'd married into it. It wasn't in her blood.

Of course, Riley had no way of knowing if any of this were true, both about her mother or about the rumors surrounding relocations. The only thing she knew was what happened within these walls. And even that she couldn't be certain of.

There was a loud groan from across the room. It rose into a trembling growl. The floor groaned as Samantha pushed her hulking frame upright. Yellow light traced over her as she crossed through the center of the room. The floor groaned again as she approached, stepping around the mostly empty water jug and dented metal cup that Riley kept next to her bed. Samantha lowered herself to one knee and then to the floor.

The feline quality of her features was still surprising: swept and tight, hair on her cheeks pointing back and down. She pointed one finger up on her right hand while her left hand hung curled in front of her. She let out a muted groan as the claw extended from that finger. She closed her eyes. They twitched as she scratched the claw across the tough skin of her palm. Her eyes remained closed as the claw retracted. Her nose ticked slightly. She squeezed her palm.

"C'mon," she said again, opening the palm again. A wide line of blood branched in her palm like streams flowing from a river. "Don't waste it."

Riley could feel the weight of the massive hand in hers, even as it was being held up. She closed her eyes and directed her face toward the open palm. The taste of dense copper almost made her retch. The sucking sound was worse.

Then, after a moment, she felt a warmth coursing from the back of her head down to her neck, shoulders, chest, arms, stomach, legs, and on to the very tips of her toes. It felt like every muscle, bone, and organ, and all the veins and connecting tissue, were a single seamless mass. It even made the sound and taste seem more pleasant. She had stepped into a warm bath.

Her eyes fluttered in satisfaction.

Samantha wiped the blood and spit from her

palm. She nodded before turning and walking away. She sat down quietly, no expression Riley could read, no words or eye contact or anything else. She was doing what she had to, whether she liked it or not.

The mom remained even when her child was gone.

Riley's eyes opened. There was no way to tell how long they had been closed, perhaps thirty minutes, perhaps five or six hours after tossing and turning for what felt like half the night. It might already be too late to catch them outside again, as they had been for the last five nights.

The room was black beyond the dissecting yellow shafts. She blinked for a moment, first to see the black outlines at the base of the wall, Samantha and Shayera's dark mounds on the other side of the room, then to make those outlines and shadows disappear. The light was a thin hue, dust from the boards still rising through it.

Neither of her companions were covered as they lay on top of their bedrolls. Shayera lay on her side with her feet curled behind her, jet-black hair contrasting with the stark and worn white walls. A slight whine accompanied her exhalations, likely from the cold coming through the window. Riley pushed evenly on the boards as she shifted her weight. Samantha faced the wall. Her heavy breathing was slow and calm, her shoulders gradually rising with air. Riley crept out from under the thin covering wrapped around her.

She carefully rose to her feet, balancing her weight to keep the floor from creaking. She made sure to distribute the pressure evenly, like standing on the balance beam, even though that was never her specialty. She crept toward the window, past where Shayera slept against the opposite wall. Snow had drifted in through the gaps in the window boards. Riley approached the light.

A white dusting over the streets and roofs, the piles of rubble, and the overlaps of makeshift windows and doors made it look like everything within the walls had been sprinkled with powdered sugar. The lights turned the snow into a massive reflector. The beams of spotlights from on top of the wall traced through the narrow alleys where buildings cast their shadows. She focused on the street, barely noticing what would otherwise have been a blinding glare from the street.

A few tracks were all but buried on the road in front of their building. Some were the long and spaced steps of wolves, the others the small and close ones of humans. Not that there was really a difference here since everyone within the wall lived as both—everyone except Riley.

Her view immediately went to the alley across the street. Snow had fallen into the nooks and gaps between the discarded shelves and other scrap lumber piled next to the building across the street. The end of a tarp fluttered again in the wind as though waking up and then falling asleep again. There was another motion.

She blinked as the light hit her eye, even though she didn't feel the sting of her iris failing to adjust. It was bright enough that it blocked out everything else, but it didn't hurt. Then it passed. A single red dot appeared in its place. Behind the plastic. Behind the pile. A pair of long ears led away from matted fur. She'd seen that same dark brown wolf every night since the last time she'd left the store—the day the guards fired their warning shot.

Her breath poured out as one long wisp. His was a faint cloud puffing as though a fire were burning on the other side of the scrap pile.

A spotlight passed over a parallel road. The wolf didn't turn away. Neither did she. It tilted its nose upward, as though just now catching her scent through the window. A white strip started just under its chin. His head angled downward, eyes becoming slits like thin slices, like the moment a cut first opens. He rose up higher, lips peeling back to reveal long fangs, one of them chipped to a sharper point than most. She could barely hear the snarl the wolf made as it stared at her. He didn't look away. The spotlight rose back up the street one block behind it.

Riley straightened up. She took in one deep breath and held it a second before letting it out in a slow mist. Five nights the wolf had been out there. He knew exactly where she was. If he was going to make a move during the night, he would have by now. She brought one hand up to near her face. She gave the wolf the finger, and he snarled once more. Riley turned away.

She checked that the others were still sleeping before carefully striding back to her bedroll. If the wolf outside wasn't going to make a move, then he was no concern of theirs. Samantha already carried enough of a burden by hiding Riley with her. She shouldn't have to deal with yet another of Riley's problems.

Riley slipped her legs into the bag on the floor and slid herself in until her neck was against the bulky puff representing a pillow. She blinked until the light cut through the shadows in front of her. The red eyes imposed over her vision as though burned in. She looked over at the nearly empty water jug, the dented cup, the few folded clothes she had, the broken-down shoes, the blade on the floor next to them, and the holstered pistol with the belt wrapped around it. Five bullets remained. Or—no more than three, really, if one were enough for Dove and another for Virgil. It wouldn't be. She eased her head onto the lumpy pillow.

She stayed like that, propped up and staring, until sleep finally took her away.

She didn't dream.

She couldn't remember the last time she had.

CHAPTER 4

FIRST OF THE MONTH. MARCH. THE NAME FELT appropriate.

Riley shuffled behind, flanked by Samantha and Shayera, as the crowd bottlenecked into the narrow opening in the wall. Rifles remained through the slits lining the exit, the barrels moving like uncoordinated oscillating fans. She made sure to keep her right hand in her pocket and the fingers loose.

She fell into step behind Samantha and ahead of Shayera as the cloud of people converged into a pair of lines and eventually into only one. She watched the feet of others slide ahead, as though every half inch gained had to be taken, as though eager to enter the gauntlet ahead. There, soldiers lined each side of the passage, all the way to the front of what used to be a high school. It was now a supply depot and barracks, and there were probably more soldiers stationed in one building than there were people in the town. The process reminded her of the traffic on the road past Samantha's house on the day most of her friends and neighbors had fled, only much smaller and more personal. The push forward stopped.

"Mrs. Wallace," said a familiar voice nearby. Riley glanced up instinctively, then back down, hoping she hadn't been noticed. The person seemed to press inward as though about to cut her off from Samantha, but stopped again instead. Riley hazarded a look.

Several gray hairs had grown into Mr. Clarkson's beard. The cold tinged his nose red. He tilted his head as a signal to go ahead.

The path opened up on the other side of the wall. The line carried on ahead with eighty, maybe one hundred people, more than half the town already moving through the passage between the fences, lining up for their portion of the monthly supplies, or how much of it they wished to take at that time while saving the rest for later. Even those who took nothing were still required to stand between the fences while the inspectors came through. Only after the entire town was clear and the south gate closed, would the west gate open. The soldiers would then enter, rush past the location where the murdered boy had fallen, and pour through the area searching every building and dwelling, checking every pile of scrap and random junk, and rifling through every possession they could find. It was basically pointless trying to keep the shop clean when a hurricane regularly came through.

"No running!" hollered one of the soldiers standing along the fence.

"Single file," said another a few places down.

They each stood about five feet apart, a step away from the fence, with their rifles angled toward the ground. The bulk of their uniforms, helmets, and masks pulled over their faces made them indistinguishable from each other. They were human mounds of armor and weapons.

It didn't matter how long it took to resupply the residents, the south gate would only open to them once every soldier had withdrawn through the west. Even if it took hours and snow poured from the clouds, as it had the month before, the people would have to stand in line, shivering and hugging their supplies, trying not to move or talk or do anything else that could be considered suspicious.

Riley kept her head down as she walked. She checked that the extra bulk under her jacket didn't bulge in any noticeable ways. Luckily the jacket was big enough that neither item poked out, it was even long enough to hide the belted holster. The pistol had become routine anytime she was outside as a less conspicuous alternative. After all, guns had been plentiful before the first exodus. Anyone could have them, and not just the antique she carried around. It made sense that some people would've been able to retain theirs even after the Guard isolated the town. The wrist blade was more obvious. It was a symbol of the Order. It had been a month since she last touched it, when she put it down following the last sweep. Leaving either weapon behind meant losing them forever. And she couldn't help feeling that she'd need them someday, just as much as she needed the other weapons Virgil had given her: guilt, grief, and anger.

The line slowed as it turned the corner into the parking lot. The outlines of individual spaces extended asymmetrically beyond the width of the passage, making the walk across the lot seem unbalanced, even more than the line of people pushing toward the fence on the right while the left was entirely empty. A couple of people used that extra space to pass or catch up with others.

“No running!” another soldier yelled from along the border. “Single file.”

Riley regained her place between Samantha and Shayera, about one hundred feet from the metal shutters that covered the school entrance. She kept the hood low over her head as she glanced at the long line in front and the steadily growing one behind. Soldiers blocked much of her view through the fence, but she could still see a few people exiting. Two men scrambled quickly along the outside of the line, one in a cap, his hands in the pockets of a trim black coat, and the other in a baggy windbreaker that bounced as he moved.

“No running!” a soldier yelled once more. It might have been the same one, but they all sounded alike. They slowed immediately, still walking quickly to pass a few others before sliding into the line. Seemed odd to rush just to wait, especially when they’d all be stuck outside for the same amount of time, but that never stopped people from standing in line to exit an airplane or cut each other off in a traffic jam. A few more trickled out before the metal-on-metal scrape of the gate closing.

Whispers among the crowd were turning into loud static. She bowed her head and steadied her breath. The town was now empty. Every person was between these fences. Thin metal separated them from the colonnade of armed guards. Nothing separated them from each other. She kept tugging at the sides and front of her hood. She missed the extra cloth she could put over her face.

The shutters squeaked so loudly as they were raised that Riley heard them from where she was in the back of the line. A small soldier placed the thick binder on the desk and straightened the ink pad and papers before sitting. "Next!" she hollered through the holes in the glass. The people at the front of the line stepped forward.

Every step took two minutes: time for the next person in line to approach the glass, give their name and fingerprint, state how much of their monthly allotment they wished to take, then either wait as the soldiers gathered their items and dumped it through the door slot, or shuffle to the other side of the fence. Either way, they would join the loose cloud of people loitering several feet from the metal door.

"Next!" the small female soldier with the mole would yell.

The soldiers nearby occasionally waved at those who had received their rations to make room for others to join their side of the passage. The line would extend, thinning out for a while, but would soon bunch up again. Straying too far from the crowd made it too easy for others to see your supplies. After the gate opened again, and they were marched single file behind the wall, there would be no soldiers to keep the predators among them from preying on the weak, the old, the isolated, or simply those who had what they wanted. Better to stay with the group, obscured, unnoticed. Everything that Riley needed.

"Next!" the soldier yelled as another person

switched from the line to the bunch. Riley kept her head lowered as she stepped forward, staying so close she practically pressed against Samantha's back. Eventually it could be time for her to change lines as well. Without a name or prints on file, Riley wouldn't have anything to pick up. She could pass on supplies, but even those who did pass were still fingerprinted. And then they'd get her. Not the soldiers. The others. The striped wolf who'd been staring at the store window all week. His buddies who mocked her and Shayera during their last trip home from the depot.

Riley glanced at the other side of the passage as another person stepped toward the glass. The guards waved at the crowd to spread out once again. Dissatisfied voices grumbled. She could have attempted to hide in the town, leap atop of a building, and squeeze behind a ledge or into a heating vent, but the consequences of getting caught would be too great. Not only for her, but for everyone.

Another step forward. Fifteen people remained

ahead of her. Movement flashed through Riley's vision. They guy in the cap and trim black coat shifted from one line to the other. He weaved up through the inside of the crowd, hidden from the guards, and joined another man who had already received his items: a single packet of food and no water. His eyes under his low cap passed over Riley for a moment as he turned his back on the ration desk. Riley followed his glance to where he was looking.

"Next!"

Another pair of eyes caught hers. The taller man in the windbreaker stood slightly out from the rest of the line, as though getting ready to jump to the other. He kept his head angled down but his eyes forward. His breath resembled a ripple of heat off a summer blacktop.

Riley imagined the white stripe and the chipped tooth. If only the man would smile or snarl. She pictured the wrinkles that emerged on the wolf's nose as it growled. She spun around to look over the soldiers along the fence next to her. Some stared blankly ahead while others watched the line through steely-eyed squints. Another soldier near the front seemed bored by it all. Would those same wrinkles appear in their human form? She felt the metal bar across her palm, the hand guard ending just under her knuckles.

"Okay, next!" called the soldier behind the glass.

Riley followed on Samantha's heels.

There was a vague resemblance between the way Samantha looked in line and how she looked while sleeping at night. Her wide hips and thin shoulders persisted, her features even more swept-back as a wolf. She was a bit thinner now with the underside of her chin hanging a little loose, as though partly deflated.

Shayera kept up behind. She was always sleek and dark, though not the pitch-black shadow she was the first time Riley saw her. Her lithe and toned build remained whether wolf or human, and the lack of enough food now showed in the visible veins in her arms. It was as though her wolf form were an exaggerated version of herself, and Samantha as well. They appeared to become more of what they already were. Or maybe not, maybe they became more of what they wished they were, with Shayera transitioning from nervous and uncertain to confident and precise. Perhaps both were true, and they simply found one form more comfortable than the other. Which would be their real selves: the wolf or the human?

Then again, maybe there was no resemblance at all. Her mind might've simply been making connections that weren't there. Not everything has a reason.

In that moment, a familiar face intruded upon her thoughts. A thin face like that of his mother, with short, dusty blond hair and wide shoulders. Those persisted. The hair became darker, more brown than blond. The face . . . she didn't see it so well. It wasn't that thin, or maybe it was. Then the blade pierced through her memory. His mouth gaped open. His wide shoulders hung as he shook, falling to the ground. His eyes faded from red to black.

She breathed as though coming up from a dive.

"Next in line." The soldier at the desk waved the next person forward. Another soldier leaned out from behind the metal door as though gauging how many people remained.

A division between the two sides remained as the loose crowd extended almost as long as the tight line. Many on both sides looked impatient and nervous, even more so for those with their supplies than without. They huddled in small groups, talking between themselves and eyeing others in distrust, in the way they couldn't while in line. Very few people had more than a week's worth of food and water. Many had nothing at all. Riley checked the fence by her side. She'd reached the halfway point between soldiers. She peeked one eye over her shoulder and nodded without knowing whether Shayera noticed or not. She tapped Samantha's shoulder.

"Moving," she whispered.

Samantha nodded slightly.

Riley took a step out of the receiving line and toward the received one.

There was a hollow bang on the glass.

"—keep us like this!" shouted the man at the head of the line.

"Sir, please remain calm," said the soldier at the desk behind the glass.

Another bang on the glass. "You're killing us!"

Riley leaned back into the line as all attention shot forward. The man wore a bright orange jacket. Riley couldn't tell for certain whether it was the man who'd come to the shop days before or not. The jackets were pretty common as there were once a lot of hunters in the town, back when there were more people and they could actually hunt.

"Sir, I'd ask you to—"

"We have a right to live!"

"Yeah!" screamed someone from farther down the

line. The two sides converged behind Riley as people leaned in for a better view of the commotion.

"We've done nothing to you!" the man screamed.

"Move away," yelled one of the soldiers along the fence.

"Back in line," ordered another.

Riley felt the crowd on the other side moving toward her, the two groups closer to merging.

Another bang on the glass.

The people continued watching, a few voicing concern, a few shouting in agreement. The soldiers called for the groups to separate. Another vibrating bang on the glass. Riley hid behind her hood, both hands in her jacket pockets, and crossed from one side of the passage to the other. She checked around her. A pair of eyes followed her before being lost in the crowd.

"We're the ones being hunted!" yelled the man at the front.

There was a loud slam against the metal door.

"Sir!" yelled the soldier now standing behind the

desk while those lining both sides of the fence waved frantically. “Back in line! Keep away! Stay in line!”

Riley felt the current of the crowd pushing forward, propelled by curiosity and anger. A sharp point tickled her back. Riley spun away from it. She pulled her hands from her pockets. A woman passed her with the corner of her ration packet angled outward. Riley turned again and faced a graying beard.

Clarkson put one hand up in front of him and pushed her shoulder. Riley brushed her right sleeve as she stuffed her hand back in the pocket. He put his hands out to shield her.

There was a crash as the metal door slammed against the fence. The crowd drew back like the tide as a trio of soldiers stepped out of the doorway. The last one slammed the door shut.

“Back!” screamed one of the soldiers within the passage.

“We’ve done nothing!” shouted a woman near the front of the line. One of the soldiers rounded on her. She cowered from the rifle in her face. He turned his attention to the man in front. The two lines parted as the other two soldiers approached. They wore the armor but not the helmets or the masks. The rifles were the same, as were the array of attachments.

"Back in line," one of the soldiers ordered as he pushed a chubby man against the people already crowded along the fence.

An arm extended across Riley as Clarkson pushed her back, sliding in front of her. She searched the crowd from behind him, catching the side of Shayera's face before she disappeared behind the others withdrawing around her. Riley craned her neck to find Samantha but didn't see her among the people lining the fence on the other side of the open passage. They looked as though they were trying to get as far away as possible from the oncoming soldiers.

Clarkson extended his arm down and across Riley's body like a seatbelt. She felt the chain links pushing against her back, even as the crowd continued to press from the front. Clarkson grabbed on to the fence next to her, locking Riley in place. A hush descended as the soldiers continued their advance.

The lead soldier scanned the crowd from under a low-sitting hat of desert camouflage. His eyes narrowed, heavy lids with cracks leading from the corners and bags hanging nearly down to his stubble-covered cheeks. She'd seen him before, during her last ration pickup with Shayera. He'd looked away then. No. More than that. He'd turned toward the other side of the passage.

She found Shayera in the crowd pressed against the opposite fence, fallen farther back down the line as though carried back up by the crowd. Samantha stood a few feet ahead, a pair of men standing in front of her like Clarkson did for Riley. One, a tall man in his forties, focused on the soldiers while the other, a teenager, possibly the other's son, watched the crowd. Riley stared at Samantha, hoping to get her attention. She shifted her attention to Shayera, whose wide eyes darted from place to place. She was almost shaking, and clearly uncomfortable. Riley craned her neck to look at Samantha again.

The lead soldier stepped into her view, the barrel of his rifle pointing the way. He stopped a moment, his head following his eyes through the crowd around him as though looking for someone. White hairs dotted his chin. The heavy eyelids, the bags, the cracks, the stubble—it all seemed so familiar, and not just from her last ration pickup. He continued on. Riley ran through her memory of her time in the Order's compound, rushing over the several dozen people who'd been cramped in there with her. No, something before that. He stopped. He looked through the crowd again. He squinted at her. He didn't look away.

"Her," he said.

Riley looked at the woman pressed against the fence next to her.

"Her," the soldier said again, "in the hood."

He pushed the crowd away to approach.

Clarkson shifted between the soldier and Riley. The soldier stepped directly toward both of them. He leaned in to see her more closely. He looked tired, almost beaten. The shadow from his hat fell over his eyes and rode over the tops of his cheeks. She'd seen the same shadow, only darker. She'd had it herself. She still could have it.

"We need to take her in," the soldier said, glancing toward the other.

Riley furrowed her brow. A nametag on the soldier's chest identified the man as "Yates."

"The girl?" asked the other soldier as he came to a stop a few feet behind the lead. He looked younger, not as hardened, less determined. "Why?"

Nametag.

"She's a threat."

Uniform.

"She's done nothing," Clarkson offered. "She's just—"

"Quiet, beast!" Yates snapped.

The other soldier cocked his head at this.

"We need to take her into custody."

"Sir, we aren't supposed to take anyone into cus—"

"She's not one of them," Yates yelled back. His stare fixed on Riley. Nametag. Uniform. He whispered, "Isn't that right, Sister?"

Riley's eyes widened with the realization.

Whispers grew around her.

Antonio's.

"My daughter didn't—"

"She's not your daughter."

The waiter.

"And she's coming with us."

The one who'd goaded Nate into attacking.

"Sir, we don't have the authority."

The one who'd made everything happen.

"We can't take her—"

Yates stepped back. He pointed the rifle toward her. Riley flinched.

The people around her pushed away. Clarkson

continued to hold her back as the fence kept her up, contained.

Soldiers along the fence stood with rifles ready. The fence shook from the fear in the crowd. She looked ahead. Past the rifle's dark barrel, she saw the tip of a blade poking out of the soldier's cuff.

"Sir!" shouted the other soldier. "We don't have the authority to—"

"The Son of Man is going as it has been determined," Yates whispered from behind the gun, "but woe to that man by whom He is betrayed."

"Sergeant! We need you over here!"

Yates took another step back, as though distancing himself from the target. From the blood of the shot.

"What's happening over there?" yelled the female soldier from behind the glass.

"My daughter isn't—"

The gun shifted to Clarkson.

"Quiet!" Yates screamed.

“What the hell are you doing?” yelled another voice over the sound of heavy footsteps on blacktop.

“Sir, this girl needs to come with us.”

“Yates,” the third soldier barked as his footsteps pounded to a stop, “stand down!”

“Sir, this girl is an immediate threat who must be dealt with.”

Riley glanced quickly to the new soldier, the three pointed stripes on his shoulder, and back to Yates, hidden behind the barrel of his gun.

“Stand down,” the sergeant said once more, slowly, with a calm force.

The lines of chain dug through the puffy jacket and into her back. Clarkson’s arm pinned her hand in her pocket and pushed the gun against her ribs. The crowd leaned away, their eyes wide with terror. She wasn’t one of them. She was one of *them*.

“Put the weapon down or disciplinary charges will be brought—”

The rifle lowered.

Riley took what felt like the first breath of her life.

Yates took another step back. The soldier behind made room for him to move.

"Charges?" Yates spat. He looked over the faces of the other soldiers, over the crowd pressed against the fence, to Riley. "Yours is not to judge." His view fixed on her.

"You need to come with us, now." The sergeant reached for Yates's shoulder. He pulled away, his focus remaining on Riley.

"The Pointed Hand passes judgment." Yates blinked quickly. His eyes disappeared behind a deep shadow. Two hands seized Yates from the side. He shoved them away.

"The Pointed Hand passes judgment," he repeated.

He threw one arm across his chest. His hand groped for the three grenades strapped to his armor. He pulled the hand away. A bright spot gleamed in

Riley's vision. A single light reflected off thin metal. Three gray pins.

"Grenade!" one of the soldiers shouted.

The crowd scattered. The fence rattled. Footsteps were an avalanche. A hard shove bounced Riley forward. There was the crunch of impact. Bodies hit the ground. Armored bodies hit together. Another hard shove took her down. She was buried.

"The Pointed Hand—"

There was a deafening boom.

Everything else was gone.

CHAPTER 5

A RINGING ROSE FROM EVERYWHERE AT ONCE.

It throbbed through the back of Riley's head. The pain followed in her chest, knees, and elbows from the impact against the asphalt. The side of her face burned where the scars and marks reminded her of the shattered glass from months before. Her hood must have lifted as she fell. Her shoulder ached as well with her right hand trapped inside the jacket pocket underneath her. She'd somehow managed to land without popping out the blade. The pain was already starting to fade while the ringing remained. She reached up to dab against the burn at her temple. Small spots of blood dotted her fingertips. She tried to move her legs. She couldn't.

The ringing ran through and over everything.

Panic surged until she felt the weight pressing down on her, against her legs, pinning her to the ground. Maybe it would be easier to stay like this. Rest for a moment. Play dead . . . or not play . . . just . . . stop. Withdraw, even if only for a minute, until whatever fresh hell had just been unleashed passed her by or, mercifully, took her down with it. Was this ever truly her fight anyway? She turned to where the noise seemed the loudest.

A woman slouched against the fence on the side of the passage. She didn't look familiar. She held both hands in front of her. The back of her hands were dotted with small, red wounds. The fence kept her up as she stared wide-eyed at herself—her hands, chest, stomach, and down to her legs. One bent sideways. The other was gone. Confusion filled her expression as she looked around, searching, finally settling a few feet away. The rest of her leg lay near a young girl who appeared to have bounced off the fence during the blast. Her eyes were open. Blood poured from her mouth. Her hair mixed into it. The woman screamed. Riley didn't hear it. She heard the ringing instead. Faint, as though far from her. It would be so much easier that way. She twisted around once more.

Salt-and-pepper hair came into view. Clarkson lay motionless on top of her. Maybe he'd decided to play dead too. She rocked to shake him. He didn't move. She reached out to nudge his shoulder. He was soft, almost squishy, and still. She pulled away, her fingers twitching. She flopped against the ground, trying to pull away. Fingers scraped the asphalt. She gave one hard push with her shoulder and rolled onto her side.

Clarkson flopped headfirst onto the ground. His eyes were open, like the girl's, glassy and distant. Blood trickled slowly from his mouth, like the girl's.

A jagged sliver of metal pierced into his ribs through the thick jacket. Fired from the grenade. Grenades. A dark stain had started soaking through the jacket. Riley slid back from him.

The nearest bodies were still. Slumped or folded over themselves, collapsed, barely bleeding, but dead. Meaty chunks hung from the fence chains torn open in the explosion. She crawled away, scraping her back against the asphalt. The people around her writhed in pain, squirming, clutching themselves in places, screaming for help or relief. A rifle had fallen to the ground where the two lines split before detonation. A hand lay next to it. Three fingers remained. Shreds of damp clothing had been tossed through the corridor.

Riley tapped at the wounds on her face again. No new blood and no old pain lingered. It was numb instead. It felt like she was floating as she pushed herself upright. She bumped into another person behind her. Looking back, she recoiled as a man stared up at her through dead eyes.

Stuff, remains, gore had all blown out, onto, and through the fence, everything contained within it, and outside large rips in the metal links. A soldier groaned several feet from the center of the blast, the sergeant with the three stripes on his shoulder. He convulsed and coughed, spitting blood with every quaking choke. His remaining hand trembled in the air. Her mind flashed to dye packs and squibs, scenes of war movies, *Saving Private Ryan*, *Full Metal Jacket*, *Apocalypse Now*. Those were her closest experiences. She knew nothing else like this. Not until now.

A wolf rushed past her, through the passage and out the breach in the fence. Another followed close behind. Then another. A low moan broke through the ambient ringing in her ears. The woman remained slumped against the fence. Her scream grew louder, as though Riley were being pulled into it. The woman's eyes were huge as she stared at the blood pouring from where her leg had been. She drew in a short breath before screaming, her hands shaking in panic. A rapid series of pops broke through the rest of the noise that flooded into Riley's senses.

Through the fence, Riley spotted a pair of wolves running toward the fence separating the school parking lot from the neighboring houses. Another series of rapid pops sounded like fireworks. Bullets shredded the pair of wolves. They dropped to the ground.

"Riley!"

Clarkson remained facedown. The young girl as well. The body behind her was face up, bent back over itself. The writhing masses cried and shouted from both sides of the passage. A haze drifted over the epicenter of the explosion like the dust filter of a camera lens.

"Riley!" she heard again.

A hand gripped her arm. It pulled her up to and nearly off her feet. She turned toward hair blacker than a shadow and eyes redder than fire. Shayera's nose darted around Riley, sniffing her.

"Mr. Clarkson," Riley said, pointing weakly in

the direction she'd crawled from. There was a sleepiness to her tone.

The ringing was gone. Growls and screams, groans and gunshots replaced it.

"Need to go," Shayera said.

Riley's view drifted over her surroundings. Around her was clear—the destruction, the bodies, the pieces of skin and exposed bones—while farther away was blurred as though she was standing on the bottom of a clear river. Shayera shook her arm so hard Riley thought it would come off. "Need to go," she said again. The fence behind her shook in long waves. Metal poles bashed and tore.

"Riley?" said another voice from over her shoulder.

A large portion of the fence to her left tilted outward. The metal links ended in ripped points. Barbed wire unspooled and broke along the top of the fence. Dark blurs streaked through the opening. Wolves ran toward the houses behind the blacktop.

A couple reached the lower fence there, leaping over before the shots rang out.

"Riley!"

Her view jostled from the shaking.

"Go right now!"

"C'mon," said the other voice as an arm looped under her other shoulder. It was human, a tear across the sleeve. Samantha held her up as Shayera pulled her back.

"I'm okay," Riley muttered. She shook her head. "I'm okay," she repeated so she would believe it. She felt the weight on her feet. She pressed the bottom of her shoes against the asphalt. The grips on her arms loosened. She blinked rapidly. The dust haze lifted from her sight. The jagged edges of ripped metal, the broken bodies, the pools of dark arterial blood, the ripped clothes, the dropped water jugs and broken bits of food packages, all became clear to her.

"Great," Samantha replied, "now let's go."

"Keep them back!" shouted a desperate voice

from outside the fence before a series of gunshots echoed off the neighboring houses. There was a whistle. A bullet sparked off the fence ahead. Samantha ducked. Riley as well.

"Go," Shayera growled, letting Riley's arm fall to her side. The black wolf bounced between the remains littering their path. She leapt through the gap in the fence.

"I got it," Riley said, pulling away from Samantha. She saw the bar lying against her palm as she pulled her hood over her head.

The two of them crouched as they slowly approached the break in the fence. Both sides had been blown out in the blast, one opening completely and the other bent outward but still attached at the bottom. A group of people stumbled over the broken side as others dashed through the opening. They ran off. Gunfire followed. A couple of them fell. The rest ran.

"Cease fire!' shouted a voice near the school.

"Hold them back!" replied another.

Soldiers scrambled around the blacktop outside the broken passage. Some people lay with their hands behind their heads, some crawled along the ground, some hustled toward the openings. Wolves darted over the blacktop, toward the fence, after the soldiers who popped off random gunshots. Some hit. Some missed. Soldiers went down. Wolves as well.

"Hurry," Samantha said as she stepped around a fallen body and toward the break in the fence. She carefully placed one foot on the chain link hovering inches off the ground. Beyond her was the open parking lot and the small fence that was never meant for wolves, which divided school property from private, then open lots, then the forest, and finally, outside of it all, the original fence around the town. The one that failed to keep the danger out.

Heavy steps rushed toward Riley. She spun to see a flash closing in. A white streak blurred up to red eyes. She braced for the hit.

Instinctively, she put out her left arm while her

right remained loose and away from her to absorb the impact on the ground while keeping the blade in place under her sleeve. The wolf charged at her. She rolled across the opening between lines. A massive claw cut the air. She tumbled over her head and backward as the claw smashed the asphalt. The wolf sprang after her, the white line down its chest heaved in short growls.

"Riley!" Samantha shouted from outside the fence.

The wolf's view flashed to the side. It circled to place itself between the two of them. Riley spotted other people dashing through the breach on the other side of the passage. Gunfire followed them.

"Go!" she yelled back.

Several wolves raced around the soldiers in the lot beyond Samantha. Shayera darted around them.

The striped wolf growled, its chipped fang peeking from under its tilted lip. Its eyes flashed away once more. Riley followed their movement. The door of the ration station was open. Soldiers poured out, the first few peeling off to the bodies blown back from the explosion, while the others drew their rifles as they moved away from the school. They stalked down the passageway. The wolf's gaze returned to Riley. It growled.

She pressed the bar against her palm. The blade seemed to sing as it clicked into place.

The hair on the wolf's shoulder shook as it drew back to strike. Riley shifted her weight. She planted to spring. The claw shot forward in an overhand strike. Its neck outstretched with the effort, shoulder extended back, exposing its throat. Riley hopped away. She tensed for a counter. A chain of gunshots rang out.

Riley hit the ground. The wolf howled in pain.

"Take him down!"

Riley tumbled forward. She sprang off the ground and dove for the gap in the fence. Her back hit the chain link, and she rolled into the barbed wire along the top. Her jacket took most of the barbs. A couple of them broke through her jeans and found her leg. Gunfire preceded a feral cry and a heavy thud. Riley pulled herself from the wire. She popped to her feet and started running.

Samantha was halfway across the lot, crouched against the back of a fallen wolf.

"You need to go," Riley said as she skidded up to her. Gunshots popped around them.

Samantha placed her hand against the wolf's back. It barely rose from breathing.

One soldier aimed at a trio of people running for the fence. Shayera tore the gun from his hand before he could fire. She ripped the gun in half. The soldier jumped in shock. She darted away.

"I'm sorry," Samantha whispered into the wolf's back.

Riley stretched over its shoulder to see its face. A black spade covered its left eye. Its breath rumbled. "No," it said as a long exhale, "I am."

Samantha rubbed the creature's big arm. Riley heard a bullet whizz past. Soldiers pushed through the gap in the fence.

"You need to change," Riley said.

One of the soldiers slipped off the end of the fence. Another pointed at where a pair of wolves had pounced on a camouflaged body.

"Change," she said again.

Samantha slumped against the wolf's back.

"We need to go."

Samantha stared up at her. Her eyes seemed to simmer. She shook her head. "Why did this . . . why . . . "

The last of the soldiers emerged from behind the fence. The one in the front waved for the group to split into different directions. Behind them, inside the broken chains, lay one naked man. A pair of soldiers continued toward Riley as others broke off, some toward where the wolves were tearing at the camouflaged body. A shadow darted in to push them away.

"Shayera!" Riley screamed.

The red eyes seemed to flash on her.

Riley waved toward the incoming soldiers, then to the neighboring houses.

Shayera jolted her long head up.

"C'mon," Riley said, pulling at Samantha's arm. "We get to the houses, out of sight, then you change, and we get the hell out of here."

"Doesn't matter."

Riley grabbed Samantha's arm.

"Nothing left."

She heard the footsteps approach, the plastic sound of the soldiers' armor.

Shayera was a dark flash toward the low fence between the school and the houses. Bullets tore through the wolves she'd left behind.

Riley tried not to pull too hard as she kept a grip on Samantha's arm.

The footsteps closed in.

"Nothing left," Samantha said again.

"You two. Don't move."

It would have been so much easier to stay there. Stay buried. But that would've been letting them win. Virgil. Dove. The Pointed Hand. She couldn't let them do that, not after everything they'd done and everyone they'd taken from her.

Riley stood as she released Samantha's arm. She raised her hands, facing the soldiers.

"That's right, miss," said one, bracing his rifle against his soldier as he reached for her, "just come with—"

Riley leapt forward. She kicked one soldier in the chest, impacting through the armor, and back-handed the other across the face. They both went down. She turned to Samantha, who slumped over, shaking.

"We need to go."

"Everything," Samantha replied. She stared up, helpless, eyes large and watery as a deer lying on the side of the road. "Gone."

"Not gone," Riley said. "Taken."

The passage between the fence was lined with death and destruction. A few soldiers still walked through, shaking their heads as they checked for survivors.

"*Sacrificed.*"

The two soldiers nearby lay motionless but breathing. Their rifles still in hand. Three grenades lined each of their chests.

"The town. Remy. Mr. Clarkson."

She'd walked through this lot hundreds of times. Bodies now littered it. Soldiers in ripped armor. Bare bodies in tattered clothes.

"Your husband. My father."

Bullet casings were sprinkled over the parking lines. Blood trickled through the cracks in the asphalt.

"Nate. Your son. My best friend."

She grabbed Samantha by the arm.

"We have to find a way to give their loss meaning."

She pulled the woman to her feet.

"Or else they *will* be gone."

She pushed ahead.

Shayera groaned as she slowed to a stop.

"You were hit," Samantha said, pointing her snout to a patch of red at Shayera's collar.

"Nothing," Shayera replied. She braced herself against a tree trunk for a moment before leaning her back against it and sliding to the ground.

"Need time."

"Let me see," Riley said, stepping up. She brushed some hair back from near Shayera's neck. Another few inches and the shot might've been fatal. The blood caked the dense black hairs. It was wet on her fingers while the hole was nearly gone. She checked the back of the shoulder. "Looks clean. Through and through," she said, recalling the phrase from a movie she'd seen, though she couldn't remember which one. Probably been a long time since she'd seen it. Been a long time since she'd seen any movies at all.

Shayera didn't seem wounded when Riley spotted her sprinting through the houses around the school and directly toward the edge of the forest. Samantha growled through her transformation while Riley kept watch. They ran too, around the houses and through the empty lots. They dodged roots and trees, puddles of melted snow, and exposed rocks for what felt like several minutes before finally stopping here, in a small clearing between the pine trees with glistening snow hanging from the needles.

"I'm fine," Shayera said, as though disappointed that she'd been wounded at all.

Samantha slumped into a patch of snow in the middle of the clearing.

Riley brushed the hair back to look at the wound again. A rim remained, but the skin was almost completely closed. "How does it work anyway?" she asked. "The healing, I mean."

Shayera shook her head. "Same as it does for you."

"If the shell got stuck in the wound then would your body push it out or heal around it?"

"Don't know. Never been shot before." Shayera sighed loudly. "They say it's a gift," she said, taking her time to enunciate the words as best as she could. "A gift from our creator."

"Creator?"

"Rerrucia, the feral god."

"God's gift," she said, remembering the words written on the wall of the murdered family, the boyfriend of the girl they'd found at the tracks. There were claws marks found on the bodies. Dense white hairs were also said to have been left at the scene. Virgil said it was a sign of the wolves'—the Canaanites as he called them—breaking their centuries-old agreement. He'd also called them "corrupted," "cursed by God," "descendants of Cain," "who'd been driven onto mountaintops and mingled with the beasts left on an already forsaken world." It had never occurred to her that the wolves—the Fenrei as Samantha called them—would have their own god. Made sense, every culture has its own creation myth, but she hadn't given it much thought.

"Who was that?"

"What?" Riley asked, coming out of her thoughts.

Shayera tilted her head in the direction they came. "The soldier."

Samantha glanced up as well, awaiting Riley's answer.

"A sleeper," Riley said, "like I was."

Samantha stared at the ground in front of where they sat.

"We were given locations and told to blend in until the call came. Yates . . . must've been assigned to take up a position in the military. Or maybe he was placed there only after I . . . "

"To target you," Samantha said, still slouched in the snow. "They hate you more than they hate us."

Riley nodded.

"Now you know how it feels," Samantha said.

Riley ran a hand through the inches of her hair. A few snowflakes fell to the shoulders of her tattered jacket. White stuffing emerged from the end of her sleeve where the blade had released.

"Did you know him?" Samantha asked, looking up once more.

"No. I recognized him from—" Riley stopped herself.

Samantha stared at her. Her nostrils flared outward from the black nose at the center of her almost bobcat-like face.

"The video. The one where . . . " She rubbed the bit of cold from her nose. "The one he chased down the street. The one who provoked him."

Samantha exhaled a low growl as she turned back to the ground. "Glad he blew up."

"It's weird though," Riley said, "the Order can't use grenades. Or machine guns. It's forbidden."

"It's not," Samantha replied.

Riley gave her a confused look. Samantha didn't see it.

"Tradition," Samantha said to the snow in front of her. "Not rule. Like the High Councilor." Her eyes rose to Riley's. "Accord says nothing about weapons. We agreed long ago, but no rule." She shook her head. "That was the Order's own in-in-ter—" Her lips twitched trying to get the word out.

"Interpretation," Riley guessed.

Samantha nodded.

"So everything that Virgil said about the swords and blades"—she patted the gun still hidden in her jacket—"and the antique pistols was all nonsense?"

Samantha shrugged. "Two hundred years. Ideas passed down." She shook her head. "Change over time." She rolled her hand at the wrist like a wheel turning. "Not always right."

"Yeah," Riley said, "I figured that out about Virgil a while ago."

Samantha sighed deeply.

Riley circled around before drifting toward another tree on the rim of the clearing. She dropped onto the dead grass in front of it. She looked over the tops of trees, the water dripping from the frozen tips of pine needles. The sky beyond was uniform gray, possible rain, snow, no way to tell. She exhaled a visible lungful of hot air. She closed her eyes.

She saw again the bodies blasted and broken against the fence. The woman, screaming upon finding her leg severed. The girl's hair, dipped in her own blood. The man, bent back and over himself. The soldier, gurgling as though drowning. How many were there? A dozen? Two dozen? She couldn't have noticed them all. And there was Clarkson. Why would he throw himself on top of her? What did she ever do to deserve that other than get a B in his freshman World History class? She wasn't even one of them. One of their kind. He must have known that. Maybe that was why he did it. To show that not all of them hated her. Some of them were good. He was good. Now he was dead. Another person dead because of her.

Riley turned away as her lip started to quiver. She closed her eyes tightly. She had to keep it in. The grief, the guilt, the anger—she needed to hold on to as much as she could. They were her weapons as much as the pistol and the blade. When the time came, she would use all of them. Virgil was right about that.

She wiped her face, sniffed, and shook the emotions away. "So where do we go now?" she asked.

The wind whistled through the trees.

"We can't stay here," she continued. "They're probably searching the valley. The army. The Order. Might have drones buzzing around right now."

There was a shuffle as Shayera rose from against the tree. "We run. As far as we can."

"No more running," Samantha replied. "This is our place. Ours. Not theirs."

Riley looked through the gaps between the trees and those in the treetops. The Order would come through the forest, but the military could come from above. Might be better if it were soldiers who caught them. Soldiers had rules, or at least the pretense of rules. They'd pulled Yates away when he threatened her. They saved her. Then he blew them up for it. That was two more dead because of her.

"I know a place," Shayera said after a moment. She stepped toward the middle of the clearing. She raised her head in a deep sniff of the wind. "West. Outside the valley."

"Can you still find it?" Riley asked.

"I know it."

"Is it safe?"

"Robert took me there. No one ever found it."

"Would he be there now?" Samantha asked.

Shayera shook her head. "Not Robert. Maybe the monster. Zarker."

A distant pop rang through the forest. Samantha and Shayera's ear perked up. Two more gunshots echoed in the distance.

"Are you ready to go?" asked Riley.

Shayera grunted, nodding.

Riley turned to Samantha. "You?"

Samantha remained slumped on the ground. She ran her hands through the shallow snow around her. She pushed down as though trying to press through the earth.

"Need time."

Samantha lowered her head to the ground. The position reminded Riley of their trip to Patrick Wallace Creek years before. She'd sat like that for several minutes at the edge of the water. It looked like a prayer form, a greeting, or a goodbye.

Goodbye.

It's said when something will soon be gone.

CHAPTER 6

THE WOODEN SHACK WOULD HAVE BEEN INVISIble to anyone who wasn't guided by smell, able to light up the world with their own sense of sight, or use some other artificial means to detect it. The drones would see it, but Riley reasoned that the snow and the distance from the town would keep them away. To anyone else, the tiny A-frame in the small clearing would look more like a mound of fallen debris than any sort of dwelling. The walls were old and cragged, gray and broken, with some planks arranged vertically and others horizontally.

Brittle, frozen sticks weighed down the roof. One long branch struck out from the side, as though broken through. The one window on the front wall was missing its glass, but without the wooden planks that covered broken ones in town. Dead leaves half-buried a corroded barrel with a "flammable" warning faded from rust exposure. Off to the side of the house, a stone well led into the ground, topped by a frayed rope with no bucket. Farther back in the clearing, behind the wall, a door and one wall were all that remained standing of what appeared to be an outhouse that the trees themselves had reclaimed as their own.

It looked to Riley like the type of place she'd roll her eyes at as the characters approached it in a horror movie. Why would anyone feel safe in such a foreboding place? The monster or undead horde or knife-wielding asylum escapee or whatever cliché villain ambling through the movie would obviously get through. Shayera motioned for Riley and Samantha to continue on. Of course, they *were* in a horror movie, all of them, only this time the monsters were the ones running. Maybe that would cancel out the rest.

The old door handle looked like it had been fashioned after a giant diamond with its color now stained to a rusted brown. When Shayera pulled the door open, it fell off the top hinge. She propped it up and motioned for the others to enter.

They were greeted by cracked and knotted walls and a floor that was as much worn planks as it was dirt. A strip of lighter gray spanned the entire back wall about three feet off the floor and twenty inches high, as though something had been there that kept the wood behind from aging with the rest. In the corner, behind where the fallen tree branch broke through the roof and angled against the slope of the ceiling, was a thick, black stove with a long pipe that led through another hole in the roof. The stove looked almost as heavy as the branch.

"When was the last time you were here?" Riley asked as she inspected the walls. Knots and grain in the wood resembled the pattern on Virgil's armoire. Whether underground or outside the city, the big piece of intricate furniture always stood out.

"Five years," Shayera replied. She crouched in front of the stove. "Little nicer then."

"Came with Zarker?" Samantha asked. She took a long sniff of the air before scrunching her nose in disapproval. Even Riley could smell it, worm-eaten wood pulp and mildew, like being buried in the pages of an old book. Nice in small amounts, but not when surrounded by it.

Shayera breathed out heavily. "Different then. Both of us. He wasn't . . . " She snorted. She shook her head. "Better not to," she said as she turned from the stove.

"Do you know where he would be now?" Riley asked as Shayera passed her.

Shayera shook her head. Pine leaves with lingering bits of white snow were clear through the open window behind her. Stars dotted the black sky. "Knew he was angry. Never knew he was . . . "

She shook her head again. Her red eyes seemed to narrow toward Riley. "He was never a monster. Not before." Shayera plopped down heavily in the corner, the wood seeming to strain from the force needed to keep her up.

"How is it?" Samantha asked, sweeping a patch of dirt from the floor with her wide palm before sitting down.

"Fine," Shayera replied. "Tired."

The fallen branch looked solid in its place, trapped between the roof and the wall, balanced as much inside as outside. It would take a great deal of force to move it in any direction. Riley leaned against the wall between the branch and stove. She let her head fall back on the soft wood.

She saw her breath as a thick puff when she breathed out. The glassless window, the hole in the roof, little gaps between the wall planks, they all let the cold in. It would be a hard night. Harder than those in the city. And without even the thin comfort of the bedroll to wrap herself in. At least it would be dark, if she wanted it to be.

"Okay?" Samantha grunted.

Riley turned to see her staring. Her red eyes were calming rather than the piercing glow of the first time she had seen them from her perch on top of the fountain in the town plaza as a line of fires blazed into the town.

"Okay," she answered.

"Not the same," Samantha said, "but one of us."

Shayera sighed a long exhale as she curled up in the corner.

"You're right," Riley said, "I'm not the same." She slid down the wall, feeling it threatening to give from her weight. "I'm worse."

Samantha slouched heavily, as she did in the forest after their escape from the town.

"I'm a traitor," Riley continued.

"So am I," Samantha replied. "So is she."

"But they didn't send anyone for you. All your people did was ask for help. My people . . . "

Samantha's head lifted. The hair above her eyes curved inward and up in a look of concern. "I don't have people. Not anymore."

Riley's gaze dropped to the floor. "Maybe if I wasn't in the town then—"

A sharp snort drew Riley's attention.

"Always happen. With you or without you." Samantha's mouth barely opened as she spoke, as though her lips were numbing in the cold. The sounds were a string of guttural noise. "Better with you."

"Maybe if I wasn't—"

"Only thing left," Samantha said, firm and certain, her eyes fixed on Riley. "All else gone."

How many had died in town? Today, or before, during the raid? How many were left now? She'd been there both times. Even before that, the day Yates . . . the waiter . . . whatever . . . goaded him into changing in front of all those people. It was the first time she'd ever seen one. It was her first proof. Virgil used it to bring her along that night to show her Zarker, the one even his own kind now condemned as a monster. Of course, Virgil provoked that attack as well. It was so obvious now. It was all a show for her, to draw her closer, play on her weakness. The injury. Her father's death. Even the murders could have been staged with claw marks carved and hairs planted on the scene. The words written on the wall.

"God's gift," she whispered to herself. She glanced up at Samantha, the soft red of her eyes still focused. "Did you mean to name him that?"

Samantha seemed to hesitate a moment before speaking. "His father did."

"Do you believe it?"

"Of him? Yes. Of this?" She put both her hands out. Short hairs rimmed the edges of the tough, scale-like skin over her palms, "I don't know." She dropped her hands in front of her. She sighed deeply.

"My parents called it a blessing. Gift. Legacy. Burden. Secret. Curse. It's . . . all of that and none."

Riley exhaled a stifled laugh. "Virgil called it punishment. Corruption."

"Mark of Cain," Samantha said. "I know." She took in one long breath as though preparing for a dive through deep water. "When I was very small, before I even knew what I was, they told me of the dawn. The time of the many gods. Plant gods. Animal gods. Gods loved by their kind. There was balance."

The red eyes rested upon Riley. She suddenly remembered the hood hovering over the top of her vision. She pulled it back.

"But there was one, name is lost. Forbidden to speak. Wanted more. Made creatures to conquer others. Vicious and brutal. Brought war against the gods. Killed them until only one was left: Rerrucia. Feral god." Samantha paused to lick and stretch her lips. "Made us before she died. Fenrei, you know." Riley nodded at the term. "Last line of the old gods. Made to blend. Hide among the creatures. Sapitus. Made to remember. Last thing left of the old gods."

Samantha nodded. A rumble rolled in her throat. "That's our story. What I remember."

Samantha's whole body seemed to droop.

"Never told him that."

Riley took a quick breath to pull Samantha's attention back. "So there was never any corruption?"

"There was. Later. Corruption is human work," she said with a slur that made Riley have to concentrate. "Twisted our stories. Made us monsters. Beasts. Lycanthropes. Werewolves." She snarled. "Canaanites."

Riley's gaze fell to the floor.

"Corruption was humans calling us 'cursed.' Remaking us to fit their story."

She could feel Samantha's eyes on her, a red glare at the edge of her vision.

"The flood, made to end their cities. Make them understand their sin. Not to punish us." The words had grown harder to understand, likely from fatigue and cold setting in. "Humans decided we were cursed. Not them. That is corruption."

Riley turned away. She looked toward Shayera at the front.

"Do you believe this?" Riley asked.

Shayera seemed to shy away.

"Ru . . . Rurrusa? Sep . . . septus? . . . septic?"

Samantha's breath stuttered as though laughing.

"Sapitus," Shayera said. "Before sapien—man." She returned Riley's gaze. "Rerrucia, feral god. Arunis, bird god. Gustinaris, beast god. They are as real to us as your gods to you."

"Stories of why we are here," Samantha said from the other side of the room. "Like yours. Your father's. It makes us feel . . . " Her mouth flexed but couldn't find the word.

Riley heard Virgil's voice in her mind, saying, "The favored of our Lord."

"Important," she offered.

"You are chosen," Virgil had told her.

"Special," she added.

Samantha nodded.

"So what do *you* think? Where did you come from?"

Samantha took a moment to stretch her lip over her teeth. "Fenrei. Sapitus," she said. "Same beginning. Different end."

"Evolution," Riley said.

Samantha nodded.

"Millions of years of genetic adaptation resulting in . . . " Riley waved her hand, searching for the correct word once more, "differences. Like humans and apes."

"Yes." Samantha kept nodding. "I never believed sapitus, humans, were evil. Corruption is using your story to diminish others. One is not born good or bad. One chooses to be good or bad."

"You?" Riley asked, turning to Shayera once more.

Shayera curled onto the floor. She tucked her nose into the crook of her elbow.

"Doesn't matter," she mumbled.

Riley turned to Samantha, who shook her head as though to say leave her be.

Virgil had called them cursed. He said they had ruined this world.

She'd never really believed everything he'd said, or even heard much of it. Not until she'd been surrounded by it every day, stuck in a tiny living space with a hundred other people espousing the same view, the same verbiage like an echo chamber. *They* were the enemy. *They* were evil. *They* had caused the ruin of the world. *They* were vile and vicious. *They* were beasts and monsters and damned creatures. Virgil made sure that was what she saw that night behind the fence of the abandoned mill outside of town. Zarker was brutal, barbaric, savage. He was everything Zarker said *they* were. All of them.

Samantha mumbled something from across the room.

Whether she believed or not, Virgil's words made Riley see them exactly as he wanted her to. Abominations. Tainted. Less than human.

Meanwhile she—*she*—of all people, was different. She was special and unique and chosen to help rid the world of these evil, unthinking, uncontrollable, unnatural creatures. His words made it easier to fight. Easier to separate *them* from *us*. They weren't people. They were monsters. They were of a lower order. She could hunt them freely. It wasn't only a duty; it was a privilege and an honor. It didn't matter whether she believed the stories about God's vengeance. The conditioning had taken hold. She'd been corrupted. And this made her dangerous. As dangerous as any of them. As uncontrollable. As much of a monster. There was no need to hesitate when she believed her cause was just.

Maybe that was why Riley always held back, even against Zarker. She had doubts.

There was a long, rumbling breath as Samantha settled onto the floor.

Riley brought the hood over her head. She took a deep breath before unzipping her jacket. As she held the end of her right sleeve, she noticed the rip where the blade had popped out. She slipped her arm from the jacket. The cold air stung her exposed skin, she felt it through her T-shirt. She pulled at the straps across the forearm. Deep impressions were left where the blade had been attached all day. She placed the weapon gently on the ground before reaching into her jacket to remove the other weapon, the one Virgil told her to use on him when the time came. She placed them both on the floor in front of her. All of her weapons, those carried on the outside and those carried on the inside, had come from him. Gifts. She quickly put the jacket back on, pulled the collar of it as high as it could go and wrapped her arms around herself.

She had been chosen. Virgil chose her. There was nothing divine about it, just one zealot's obsession with destroying those he believed less worthy than him. From that first night, the accident, to this one, the attack on the settlement, the only plan has been his.

She closed her eyes. She tried not to picture the

bits and body parts launched across the passage between the fences. Clarkson motionless on the ground on top of her. Her mother driving without looking back. The shattered glass and red streams flowing from her. Remy hanging there, thick blood dripping from the contours of his face. The diamond tip of the blade poking through. The life leaving him. The boy she'd known since they were both little. Both still dealing with the same loss. Now he was lost to her. She couldn't stop from seeing these episodes from her life, from remembering them. But she could change the image.

She could imagine a different face above the throat the blade emerged from. She pictured the outward cracks on Virgil's face shattering, the white tail of his hair pulled back below the blade, the one on the floor right in front of her. Forget the gun. Too impersonal. She wanted to feel the life leave his body. She wanted to make him feel the same terror her best friend had before he died. She could at least picture that instead.

That was the second thing Virgil had been right about. She would end the corruption.

It felt like she'd been staring at the inside of her eyelids for hours. In the dull black she saw everything she'd told herself to forget, over and over. Over and over.

A thin light filtered through the glassless window at the front of the cabin. Her neck was stiff from her head tilting down to the floor. Her back ached from the hard wood against it. Minor pains, quickly faded and forgotten. It was other wounds, those she couldn't see, that she'd carry with her. Over and over.

There was a rustle from the front of the room. Shayera stirred on the floor ahead. Samantha remained curled almost fetal on the floor. For months she'd tried not to remain in her altered form for too long. Only at night, when the floodlights went on and the temperature dipped. Shayera didn't seem to mind, but Samantha, she'd hidden it. Even from her own son. Here, in the woods, with her only set of clothes shredded after her turn, she'd probably have to stay like that. It couldn't be easy to be forced to live as something you'd spent most of your life denying even existed.

Riley pushed up from the ground. Tired as she was, there was no sense in even pretending that sleep would come. Shayera seemed to sense this motion as she too arose. Her eyes were bright red. The rest of her was shadow. Riley allowed her to remain that way.

"I should go," Riley said quietly, knowing Shayera would hear her, hoping Samantha wouldn't.

The wolf turned away from this.

"They came after me once. They'll do it again."

A rumble from Shayera's throat.

Riley looked to Samantha once more. She could hear the long, relaxed breaths. At least there could be some kind of peace, however short. "Keep her safe,"

Riley said. "She's already . . . " Shayera stared at her through the corner of her eye. " . . . She's suffered enough. She doesn't need to lose any more."

A grunt.

The metal of the weapons was ice on her fingertips. She opened her jacket. Straightening her fingers, she pressed them together to once more strap the blade to her arm. As she tightened the two straps into place, the skin protested that not enough time had passed since the weapon was last worn. She looked over the weapon: the simple sleeve that covered the back of her arm almost up to the elbow, the long and flat sheath running the length of her forearm, the metal plate over the back of her hand, the bar that wrapped around, and the long button over her palm. Might work after yesterday. Might've been damaged as they ran. She picked up the gun. One chamber remained empty. It had been so long since she'd fired it at Dove. Might not work either. Probably best to test it but that would be a waste of a bullet. The blade though. She squeezed her hand shut. The blade popped out.

There was a soft growl from near the door. Riley felt Shayera's stare.

Riley released her hand to let the blade retract. She tucked the gun into her interior jacket pocket, carefully slid her arm into the sleeve, felt a slight tug as the straps caught the interior lining, and zipped the jacket shut. Frayed ends hung from where the blade had pierced the sleeve. Nothing she could do about that. Maybe she could find a new jacket, somewhere.

"Yes," Shayera said, "you should go."

The red eyes looked away when Riley turned toward them. There was a deep, rolling rumble.

Riley stood, distributing her weight evenly to keep the floorboards from creaking loud enough to wake Samantha. She'd only want to stop her. Better she leave while she could. Samantha and Shayera could find some place to go. West, maybe three or four hours running. Shayera seemed human enough when she wanted to be, and her slim build and sharp features would probably help when she was a bit awkward. Good looks were the best excuse. Maybe they would even find others who'd fled from Stumpvale . . . Wolfland . . . the settlement . . . whatever it was called. Better without her. Better without the Order . . . the Pointed Hand . . . following them just to get at her.

Samantha took another long breath in her sleep. Her ear twitched.

Riley felt Shayera's gaze following her across the room. She reached for the door, the fake glass diamond on the handle, clear on this side without the weathering on the other. She lifted the door as she pushed it open, and it groaned with the motion. Riley stopped to look back. Samantha didn't move. Shayera's eyes tensed, carving red slivers into her black shadow. Riley stepped out. She pushed the door behind her, closed enough that it held out the light, not enough that it would make a sound.

Riley brushed a few brown needles aside before

taking another step. She slowly, cautiously, walked into the woods alone. It was better this way. Samantha had already lost everything she had. She'd seen the people she loved taken, over and over. Over and over. She didn't need to go through that again.

Riley continued her slow march until the cabin was barely visible through the trees encapsulating her. She watched her breath float up and away. Rubbing her heavy eyes, she tried to remember the way they'd come the day before. She took a couple of quick steps. The muscles of her legs were tired but strong. She was no longer broken. She'd become more than she ever imagined.

CHAPTER 7

ANOTHER ARMY TRUCK PULLED OUT FROM behind the school. It jostled over the grooves carved as long tracks into the ground, over where the students used to eat lunch and play baseball during PE classes. The truck continued around the narrow road that circled between the back of the school and the houses lining the border of the forest. A series of posts were all that remained of the fence separating campus from the outside world, or what she and her classmates would've called freedom.

Riley remembered sitting in that grass and

looking at those old houses, the faded green one with the high chimney and wooden fence around a nice little yard with flower boxes in the spring, a lamp next to the entrance, and a faded American flag in the front window. Some days the garage would be open to show the back end of a wide Cadillac, the chrome sparkling far more than seemed normal. They'd joke that it looked like the type of place that Henry Hill would've been relocated to at the end of *Goodfellas*. They started referring to the owner as Henry. Half of the posts on that wooden fence had been knocked over. The backdoor of the house was bashed in.

The truck rounded campus before joining the main street. Under the canvas top, Riley could see soldiers seated and facing each other, rifles crossed over their laps. She squinted to see boxes farther inside with the letters MRE in red, tiny in the distance. The truck turned away from the direction of the wall. It passed another identical army truck following the same path the first did minutes before, another pickup for the supplies soldiers pulled from the rear of her old school.

She had started by retracing their steps from the night before. They'd gone almost exactly east and only slightly south, over the rim of the valley. She'd reached the ridge of the mountains within minutes at an easy run. The town was visible through the trees, and she'd dashed just under the ridgeline. She spotted the school to the south of town, leading east to Big Bridge then northwest to the museum. Several metal structures sat on the grass of the park, remaining vague even as she rushed closer to the town. Probably construction equipment, she'd figured: things that made it possible for the black wall to be built so quickly. The wall itself carved through the area between the school and the bridge. Closer, blackened buildings marked the path the Order had taken from the west, parallel to the path she'd taken from her place behind Mr. Crawford's house. Armored vehicles guarded the plaza at a few checkpoints on each side of the town, while concrete blocks closed off several other intersections—as if anyone who wanted to escape would have used a car. Hell, it wasn't like anyone who wanted *in* would've used one either, as they'd all seen. She'd moved into the valley closer to the school, easily leaping the half-hearted fence the National Guard never finished and losing the town behind the trees until, finally, emerging within sight of houses behind the school, seeing the first so far of four trucks removing the remnants of the army's failure.

The soldiers had to know there was a possibility of someone returning to view the town from within the forest, but they didn't seem to care. They waved for yet another large truck to back onto the concrete between lunchroom benches and start loading boxes into the back. The rear of the school was a patchwork of hasty repairs, windows covered by boards spray painted with square-shaped logos she couldn't identify from her distance. Heavy tire tracks tore wide loops into the grass. Soldiers trailed out of the building, more than she'd ever noticed before.

Where were they during the chaos? When the very people they were supposed to be protecting actually needed protection?

She sprinted away, west, in the opposite direction of the way the three of them had come the day before. She weaved around the trees and roots several yards into the forest. She cut into the town, ducking between the same houses she and Samantha used as cover.

Of course, the wall remained completely untouched. Maybe a few of the inhabitants had been recovered, replaced within the confines. Although, given how swift the army had been to remove their supplies, if anyone had been recovered, they weren't staying.

Riley ducked against the rear wall of a house bordering the parking lot. The backdoor was gone and the windows had been shattered long enough that mold had begun to grow in the carpet inside the door. She checked the room. Books had been tossed off the shelves, the couch overturned, and the television ripped off the wall. Dead leaves and grass had blown in through the openings. She snuck through the back to the front of the house, pushing away the glass from the front window as she positioned herself under it.

Several soldiers inspected the area where the fence had torn open the day before. Others walked through the passage from the school to the town. They did so easily, without worry. Until yesterday, she'd never seen a single one of them step foot between those fences. The damage was the only sign she could see of any Order activity in the town itself, although she had yet to pass the old underground compound on the other side of the town, in the direction she'd be going on her way back to her apartment. She hadn't expected her "quick foray," as Virgil had called it, to end in weeks of imprisonment. It had been three months. Hopefully, Mr. Crawford hadn't carted her possessions to the curb.

"My God," she heard one of the soldiers remark, "is this what they did?"

The soldier stood in the opening torn through the fence. Spots of gore remained on the chains and in the cracks and ridges of the asphalt while the bodies, clothing, and belongings had all been cleared. Perhaps they'd be examined and experimented on, but that was a different concern.

"Heard they started pounding on the glass just to pull the guards out," said another soldier, stepping around the first, "and that's when the panic started."

The first resumed his path down the passage and toward the entrance into the wall. "They can do this, should put 'em all down. All of 'em."

The other soldier grunted as they continued across the parking lot and toward the turn before the wall.

The official report would make no mention of an outsider infiltrating the army's ranks. Of a lone, radicalized agent using the military's weapons for his own means. Such information wouldn't fit the official narrative of the savages who needed to be contained at gunpoint. Clean it up before leaving. Make it nice for the cameras that would inevitably come. Sell the story to ghost-town tourists on summer vacation.

She'd seen what she needed to: the town, abandoned by its people, and soon by the soldiers who'd held those people there. It was time to move on, gather what she needed, and prepare for what she knew would come, whether she wanted it or not.

The glass crushed under Riley's feet as she left. She'd be gone before anyone who heard the sound could react. There was no more reason for caution, no reason to look back. The soldiers clearly didn't want any trouble. They'd tried. They'd failed. They'd probably be gone the next day with nothing but the wall and the broken fence to show they were ever there. Nothing but ghosts and memories would remain. One unseen and one slowly rewritten over time. That was the plan.

Everyone, everywhere she'd been, always had a plan. It was theirs, of their own thinking and creation. Plans were the work of man. God, or gods, couldn't care any less.

CHAPTER 8

IT SEEMED ALMOST IMPOSSIBLE FOR THE UNFINISHED supermarket to appear even more empty. No cars in the lot, no light through the glass, and blown snow piled against the side of the building, looking more like an abandoned supermarket rather than an incomplete one. Hopefully there'd at least be something left. Something she could use.

Riley strode confidently to the front doors. Streaks on the facade marked where ice and snow channeled down from the roof. Tiny droplets of frozen water clung to the edges of the unnaturally frosted windows and handles of the front door.

She stopped at the door. It was probably easiest to break the glass here. Either the blade or the cuff itself could do the job. The scars on her face and arm seemed to radiate a dull throb at the idea of shattered glass cascading all over her. She searched for another way around, any other entrances she could climb to, or even a trash can she could launch at the window like Spike Lee in *Do the Right Thing*. No cans or newspaper boxes, not even any large rocks. She pulled her jacket sleeve over her palm to wipe dirt from the window in one of the doors. She lowered her hood and pressed her ear to the glass. Not even the hum of electricity came from inside.

She stepped back and took one look at the street across the parking lot behind her with the empty land of bare trees and sparse grass. She took a deep breath, gritted her teeth, and launched one foot to the spot where the two doors touched. Her injured leg—the one with the fat scar that still ran up the back. That wound would never heal. The metal shook the glass in their frames. The metal held but dented. She kicked it again, faster but not as hard. The metal bashed together loudly. Another kick vibrated through her entire leg. The doors flew open with a metallic clank. A bolt several inches long barely missed her—it fell almost exactly where another bolt had been broken off inside a hole in the floor. She checked around her once more. The bare trees and sparse grass didn't notice her.

A shaft of early afternoon light shining through the broken doors did little to brighten the far reaches of the large, empty room. She blinked and her vision cleared immediately. Even through her jacket, she felt the chill of the room. She walked across the empty floor. The same scrapes and scratches stood out, the same marks and scuffs on the columns. She listened for a buzz of electricity but heard only her own soft footfalls on the linoleum tile. The elevator in the back wouldn't be running. She continued toward another pair of doors directly opposite those at the front. Large scrapes led from the door to the elevator nearby. Unlocked, the doors opened into a storage area with loading-dock doors big enough for the trucks she'd seen hauling soldiers and supplies to back into. The ground was rough, with deep scratches funneling toward the doors behind her and in another direction, toward another, single door on the opposite side of the building from the elevator shaft. There had been beds to haul, dressers, weapons from the barracks, and Virgil's armoire. They'd probably have been extra careful with that. On the other side of the single door was a staircase. Flecks of dirt dotted the exposed concrete of the steps.

She ran her hand along the wall as she climbed. She connected the dots of dirt into boot prints up the staircase to another door at the top. Unlocked again. A small room opened before her.

The hanging head of Christ greeted her. The wooden beam of a crucifix started halfway up the wall and nearly reached the ceiling. The crossbeam was wider than she was. Real nails held a partly painted bronze Jesus in place against the wood. Traces of red paint dotted his hands and feet, and fell down his face like tears. He seemed to stare down at the altar beneath him. Several rows of candles were stacked on the top like theater seats. Solid wax dripped from some while others were untouched blocks with clean wicks. As she approached, a small picture placed between the upper two rows of candles came into sight. The faded black-and-white photo displayed a woman's profile peeking from under a dull blue headscarf. Mary. The photo's corners had worn off with age. Riley plucked the picture from its place. The texture was rough against her fingers. She turned it over and read the neatly handwritten words: "Only after the Last Judgment will Mary get any rest; from now until then, she is much too busy with her children."

Riley placed the photo back between the rows of candles and stepped away for a better look at the altar. She opened each of its four drawers one by one. They contained nothing but dust and one half-empty pack of matches.

Words pulled her attention to her left. She craned her neck to see them, shuffling back to bring the message fully into view. The letters stacked one next to the other, each a monolith on its own.

The Pointed Hand Passes Judgment.

Anyone who came through the door behind her wouldn't be able to avoid seeing those words every time they passed. Whether they read the words aloud or not, they would echo in the person's mind, over and over, over and over, until they became true. Until they became their own.

Nothing but furniture was left in the barracks. No cloaks, no shirts or pants, not even a single pair of shoes, only neatly made beds, empty drawers, and a trio of hooks stuck into the wall at each person's station. She growled in frustration. Riley continued through, cautiously, listening for any unknown sounds and leaning out to check around corners before moving on.

The weapons closet was open. The cases were intact, closed, and empty. Enough weapons to arm a small, albeit antiquated army, and they were all gone. "Damn," she muttered. She'd come all this way only to find emptiness.

The final door in the hallway was also left open. A compulsion seemed to draw her past every other closed door lining the passage and directly to Virgil's office on the far end. As she approached, a small gap between the door and the frame came into view. The urge to move forward grew even stronger. For the first time what he wanted her to do was the same as what she wanted. She tightened the sleeve around her right wrist to muffle the click of the blade as much as possible before releasing it. Even that tiny motion seemed to sing in the silence. Holding her blade hand up and pushing gently with the other as she peeked from behind cover, she slowly . . . cautiously . . . listening for even the tiniest sound . . . pushed the door open.

Empty. She withdrew the blade on her wrist. Not only empty but spotless. The chairs were perfectly aligned. No residual water remained in the sink basin of the bathroom. The bed was neatly made with the sheet tucked in and the single pillow symmetrical to the sides. Everything was perfectly in place. Except the armoire. It was a shock of rich color among the bland. It was intricate among the simple. It called out to her. She reached for the small, golden handle. The lock banged between the two panels.

This too would be part of his plan. A trail of open doors and closed distractions had led to this last locked place. Locked doors were always more tempting.

She looked over the rolling and rising contours that crossed freely over the pair of panels covering the armoire. As many times as she'd stood in front of it, as many times as she glanced over or plainly stared, she could never find the image in its design. Everything Virgil had done—appearing on benches throughout the town, pushing her friend exactly where he'd need to be to cause her accident, being there when she woke up, feeding her just the right information to make her join his cause, making her first encounter with a wolf be one that fit his description, making her watch as he burned through her town and murdered her best friend, even, possibly, engineering her escape from Wolfland, and finally leading her through this last maze—*everything* was planned to get her to this spot.

Traces of glue remained from the tape used to close it during the move, but nothing else tainted the image before her. She nearly brushed her cheek against it looking over every inch of the design, every hill and valley of the wood. She moved away again. No clearer image appeared. It was chaos among the balance. Maybe that was the point. Maybe this was here to make her analyze, make her think that this design had been chosen. Chosen like she was. Maybe it was here to remind her that no matter how far she'd distanced herself from him and his thoughts, she was still under his control. Still doing his bidding. Or maybe it was just an armoire. Just a dumb piece of furniture. Another obstacle between her and where she wanted to be.

"And behind door number one," she said to herself. There was a sharp crack as she ripped the lock out of the wood.

Shirts hung on clothes hangers. They sparkled several shades of white. A wooden cane with a bronze handle shaped into a lion's head rested between a set of drawers and the side of the wardrobe. She pulled a pair of black boots from the corner of the wardrobe. She sighed as she saw the length of the foot, she'd be sliding as much in oversized shoes as she was in the broken ones she already had. She chucked the boots back into the closet where they banged against the wood. Several folded pairs of pants were lying atop the four drawers spanning three-quarters of the cabinet's width.

She pulled open the top drawer. Books with faded spines rocked from the force. Different versions of the Bible, the writings of Thomas Aquinas, St. Augustine of Hippo, Joseph Butler, and other names she didn't recognize but assumed were other religious scholars, were separated by notebooks with strings tying them closed. She grabbed one of the books. The string pulled open easily. The handwriting inside shifted from neat and lopping to scrawled and feverish and back. The words *corruption* and *curse* stood out among the densely packed pages. *Father* caught her eyes, dug sharply into the page as though written with a razor. She flipped ahead in the book. A clump of pages turned to reveal one page.

"Reread Exodus 21:17. 'And he that curseth his father, or his mother, shall surely be put to death.' I am waiting."

"'I am waiting,'" she repeated to herself, imagining the quote written down the barrel of the pistol pressed against her side.

She placed the notebook on a pair of pants and pulled out another. The same changes in handwriting were repeated here through notes on Aquinas, Augustine, and the others. *Curse* reappeared over and over, along with *redemption*, *penance*, and *punishment*. Lines and entire pages were quoted and analyzed. She skimmed a handful of pages, reading observations on interpreting the ideas of damnation and salvation, and searching for some proof of forgiveness. She looked over the other notebooks still left in the drawer, each one as dense as the first. It would take days to look through them all, and she probably still wouldn't understand all they contained. The notes ended with that same quote: "And he that curseth his father, or his mother . . . "

She dropped the second book on top of the other. Whatever he wanted her to find wouldn't be buried on a random page in one of eight notebooks. He'd laid his breadcrumbs too clearly to let them be lost now. He also probably knew she'd have little patience for his religiosity. She placed the two books back and closed the drawer.

The contents shuffled as she yanked open the next drawer down.

She chuckled slightly. "Of course," she muttered.

Inside, a lone notebook sat on top of a single file folder. There was nothing else. That was it. This was what he wanted her to find.

She opened the book. A newspaper clipping started to slide out before she caught it. The brittle paper had no date and described the creation of the relief wall in front of the Natural History Museum. The same handwriting altered in extremes from elegant to nearly illegible. Long lists of names stretched down the page, some scribbled out, some with notes attached. A few were marked with the word *potential*, a few with *legacy*, but that word was rare and occasionally crossed over with *blood* in its place. *Cursed* was the most common. The ink changed as the pages went on, the passage of time apparent in the changing pens he used. Names began to stand out. Greg Clarkson and Elizabeth Wald were on the same page. *Cursed* was written next to their names. Cynthia Reece, her gymnastics coach, had *potential* written next to hers. Francis Wilson, the school principal, had no note. Diane Ellis, Sister Kennera, each had *potential* scratched out and *blood* in its place. Patrick Wallace: *cursed* in large letters and circled, *sacrifice* added in bolder, newer writing. Harold Collins, who could be Nate's friend Craig's dad: no note. Clarence McKnight: *chosen* in large letters and circled. "Martyr," Riley read aloud from the newer writing in the book. Samantha Chavis—*Could that be Mrs. Wallace?*—*cursed*. Amanda Martin . . .

Riley paused. She hadn't seen her mother's maiden name in years. *Legacy* was written next to it. The names ended shortly thereafter. They picked up on the next page. Large circles obscured the names surrounding that of Sandra McIntyre. *Potential* was again scratched out, with *chosen* written above it. The names again ended soon after that.

"McIntyre shows tremendous potential," read

one of the lines written in a quick, sharp hand, as though trying to get the words out before they were forgotten. More notes about "the McIntyre girl" continued down the page, her beliefs, her attendance at church and school, her habits. There were notes on her parents, Benjamin and Dolores McIntyre, their habits and characters, and a boy as well, Ben Jr. Another newspaper clipping poked out from in front of the next page.

The clip told of the murder of the McIntyre family. Found in their house on Tanacross Avenue, Big Bridge road. There were few details of the killing other than that the bodies had been found in one room with blood trails indicating they'd been brought there from elsewhere. "The Baileys," Riley remarked. The couple's eleven-year-old daughter, Sandra, had been away at the time. Before Dawn Musgrave it had been twenty years since Stumpvale's last murder. Here they were, the same method, the names of victims, written in a notebook right in front of Riley's eyes.

She felt her adrenaline rising, her heartbeat growing. She wanted to toss the book away as though touching it somehow leaked evil into her fingers.

The exposed page followed the development of Sandra McIntyre after the death of her parents and brother. It read of how she'd been taken in by social services and placed with a new, foster family, Matthew and Ashley O'Banion, who'd led her to an active role in the local church. Riley paused a moment before flipping back several pages. She scanned for the name. Matthew O'Banion, with the words *potential* and then *blood.* Ashley Popov: *legacy.* Sandra McIntyre, only survivor of the last set of murders in the town, had been placed with members of the Order. Riley remembered there being another victim at that time. More names continued on the next page. She skipped most before coming upon Gladys Benally—*Shayera*, Riley thought—*cursed.* Then Jonathan Yates—"Yates," Riley growled—*legacy* replaced by *blood.* And the next, Robert Zarker—Riley snarled—*cursed.*

Sandra McIntyre's story continued in a fresh pen on a new page. She showed tremendous potential and dedication to their cause. Riley's eyes paused once more upon the name Father Pius. He was impressed with her but cautious. She seemed a bit too zealous in her training. Nonetheless, he had accepted her into the Order under Virgil's tutelage. She had been given the name of Sister Dove.

Sandra McIntyre disappeared from the pages that followed. There was only Dove. The blood had done something to her. She moved like no one else, rivaled only by the Prior himself. She was unquestioning, loyal, devoted, but there was something else as well. She had taken to an odd habit—giggling during training as if she were excited by the violence. She once had to be restrained after nearly beating a sparring partner to death with the hilt of that partner's wooden training sword. She'd also confided to her parents that Jesus spoke to her during her nightly prayers, saying that she'd been chosen to lead a great nation.

The account continued on to an event at Sandra's school, where officials found a dead cat in a metal case in her locker. The cat was missing one paw, one ear, and both eyes, all crudely cut from its body. She told her teachers that the cat was a sick creature, and she believed its blood would help it heal. The principal asked why she believed this. "It's the Lord's way," Sandra had replied. The Prior, Father Pius—Riley's father—threatened to excommunicate the girl for "dishonorable conduct" and "threatening our secrecy." Sandra was removed from school after this and brought directly under Virgil's tutelage.

A large block of text was scribbled out so heavily that Riley couldn't see the lines even as she leaned closely to read them. "Sister Dove has proved an invaluable asset, far too precious to ever be cast away," read the following sentence, "but she is not worthy."

The names picked up again. Riley recognized some from school or other places in town. There were the girls on her gymnastics team, Nate's friends

Craig Collins and Tony Miscone. The word *sacrifice* appeared newer than most next to the names Dawn Musgrave and Liam Bailey. Remy Esplin jumped out from on the next page. *Sacrifice.*

Riley felt her teeth grind. Is that all he had been? A sacrifice? An acceptable loss in whatever monstrous game Virgil had been planning for all these years? Is that all any of these people were?

"He didn't even know," Riley muttered to no one. "He was harmless."

Her eyes drifted lower on the page. Nathaniel Wallace: *cursed.* Fresh ink read: *sacrifice.*

Her eyes fell closed. She felt her lip beginning to quiver and her eyes tear up. It had been her fault. Her fault that he was gone. Targeted for no reason other than being her friend. That was all. She took a deep breath, squeezed her eyes shut and her mouth closed. She'd known this already. She'd already chosen how to deal with it. She'd held her anger in this long; she could continue until the time came. Until she was face-to-face with the real monster. She blinked and turned away and wiped her sleeve over her eyes. The rip from the blade caught her focus. She turned her hand over to see the little metal bar which crossed over her palm. She saw her shadow reflected between the grime that had accumulated over the last few months. She blinked again until her eyes cleared.

Riley McKnight, circled. *Legacy*, crossed out. *Blood. Chosen.*

Hers was the last name written on the page.

She turned to a pair of newspaper clippings.

Fatal Accident Claims City Councilman.

The other had no headline. It was only an obituary. Her father's.

She didn't need to read them. The true stories were handwritten behind them.

She felt herself tremble as the words unfolded before her like a confession. High Councilor Wallace, a favorite of Father Pius, had put up a noble fight, claiming a pair of martyrs and severely wounding Sister Dove, which required Virgil himself to step in and finish off the weakened beast. Sister Dove was in dire condition, having nearly lost her leg in battle. "I pray she survives," he wrote, "but if God chooses to take her home, may she take her place among the knights of Heaven, for her ignorance does nothing to belie her righteousness."

The story then charted her recovery, her adjustment to the new prosthetic fitted for her, admiration in how she had denied the use of more modern replacements for one suitable to their restrictions. "Her devotion cannot be broken," he wrote. Interspersed with her story was that of Father Pius's slow but inevitable decline as he refused to receive sacrament from any but his fallen friend.

"Our effort in clearing way for new leadership will soon prove fruitful. We will usher in a new age of purity and beauty to the land. No longer will this curse be allowed to exist with impunity. Sin will be punished. I will—"

Riley twisted away with disgust. She panted, eyes flashing over the bare walls around her. It seemed as though she'd been drowning, and only now, pulling away, pulling from Virgil's world, was she safe. Safe. Not that she'd been that way . . . ever.

The scumbag had engineered her father's death. Of course, he didn't have the courage to take him on personally, so he instead used his orphaned, disturbed lackey to murder the High Councilor. He did that in order to cut off her father, his leader, from the blood that sustained him through the strain of fulfilling his duties. Her mother had warned of the consequences of withdrawal. The aneurysm had been a cover-up, like Patrick Wallace's car accident. It was a way to keep the town from panicking, dividing itself into all-out war—like the exact war that inevitably came. The beast had chosen the slowest, most painful way to remove his rival from leadership. Coward couldn't even do it himself.

"You monster," she muttered through clenched teeth.

Father Innocent the Fifth was already in ill health

before taking over as Prior. Virgil estimated no more than five years before he would ascend to leadership. He had already chosen his name: Vigilius the Thirteenth. "To redeem the name itself for its part in the abysmal agreement which has allowed this corruption to exist."

Riley had become withdrawn and sullen after her father's death. She had stopped attending church, which would make her hard to reach. However, she'd taken to wearing her father's old military clothing, a sign that she not only sought to be close to him but also had a positive association with order and command structure. She would make a good soldier.

She'd also taken to spending time with the son of the fallen High Councilor and his successor, who had withdrawn from both local and public life following the death of the leader of the cursed. This could make her more sympathetic to their cause. It could soften her.

There were notes about her involvement with

gymnastics on a local and state level, her first ankle injury, her preference for old movies and her relationship with the "Quaker boy" from outside of the town. And there were many notes about her friendship with Nate. How they'd become nearly inseparable in the years following their fathers' deaths. It was as though fated, "too perfectly crafted to be serendipitous. The offspring of the fallen leaders appear to be in exact succession of their progenitors." There was even a description of the two of them, of her and Nate—the name sprung casually to her mind—sitting on the bench outside of her apartment building, looking as though they had become aware of him, Virgil, standing in the shadows nearby.

"It appears as though neither the cursed nor the chosen are aware of their roles. The McKnight girl may yet be salvaged if a suitable fission can be driven into the friendship. She would need to be convinced."

What followed was Virgil's own description

of the events of the accident, although it could no longer be called that. Her eyes traced over it, yet none of the words entered her mind. Instead, she saw the road ahead, the turn approaching a bit too fast but no more than usual. She heard the pop, the screech, the crunch. She saw the world flip upside down and the cascade of glass.

She shook her head. She squeezed her eyes shut and flexed her jaw. She waited until she felt herself calming once more. She'd lived this before, all of it. She survived then. She could hold it in now. She would use it later.

She knew the story from there on: how Riley's lack of faith would make it more difficult to make her devote herself to the cause. Instead, he would use Sister Kennera to reach out to her, her injury to draw her into what the Order could offer, and the emptiness of her father's death to finally hook her into joining.

Virgil wrote of Riley's fascination with Sister Dove and the competitive stubbornness she had in training. He pushed her away to bring her closer. Told her she couldn't join so she'd want nothing more than to do so. He'd used sacrifices—"sacrifices"—to convince her of the danger of the Canaanites and to pull her closer to the cause while pushing her away from the cursed.

"The McKnight girl shows greater skill at this point than even her predecessor. She could one day even surpass her father to become the greatest of us. She may be the one to end this curse."

The next page began, "She has taken the name of Sapphira."

Nothing followed.

She trembled as she closed the book. She let it drop from her fingers and into the open drawer of the armoire. The hit echoed off the file folder. She stood blinking at it for a moment, forgetting it was even there as she'd lost herself in the pages of Virgil's confession. There was a large crease in the middle of the folder from being folded along its length. This was the last thing he wanted her to see.

The folder smelled vaguely of smoke. One thin sheet of paper stuck to the cover for a moment before detaching and drifting to rest in front of her. A printed form of a birth certificate. James Henry Payne, born June 23, 1942, in Stumpvale, Alaska. Son of Cian Abraham Payne from Larkhall, Scotland, and Annalisa D. Steffensen from Hotstebro, Denmark.

At the bottom of the paper was a round stamp, unevenly printed. She recognized the seal at the bottom of the paper as that of the Accord: triangular rays extended from a round sun rimmed by the words, "Nobilitate Nobis—By the blood we are bound." She remembered the last time she had been in this room, in the days preceding the raid. Wolves marked their birth certificates with the seal of the Accord. He must have taken it during the attack. 1942. Riley furrowed her brow at this. She looked over the names once more. A series of impressions poked from the back of the page. Riley turned it over.

"Sister Sapphira," it read in the neat handwriting she'd seen in the notebooks, "find me in the place where you found yourself. If you are worthy, make me the last sacrifice. If you are chosen, bring me my fate. We are the Pointed Hand. Let this be our last judgment."

James Henry Payne would be old by now. An old man. White haired. An old wolf. Riley felt as though a weight were pressing her down as the words came back to her. Words carved into the barrel of the gun she concealed in her jacket. Words written by hand. "And he that curseth his father, or his mother, shall surely be put to death." He'd added, "I am waiting."

An acrid taste filled her throat. She shook as though about to vomit. She choked it back down. She slammed the folder shut in front of her. She crushed in her hand. James Henry Payne, born 1942. Cursed. Father: Cian Abraham Payne. Mother: Annalisa D. Steffensen. There was only one reason he'd leave that record for her. "And he that curseth his father, or his mother, shall surely be put to death." She threw the crumbled file folder at the ground.

I am still waiting, he had said.

She slammed the armoire door. It bashed against the open drawer. She slammed it again.

Make me the last sacrifice.

She yanked the drawer from the dresser. She threw it across the room. It broke against the blank wall. The notebook flew out.

Bring me my fate.

She slammed the armoire door again. She kicked it until it splintered and broke off the hinges. She roared, tearing the other door with one vicious pull.

He cursed his father and mother. He wants to die.

She stalked to the chairs in front of the desk. She grabbed one and spun as she launched it across the room. It didn't matter where it hit as long as it broke.

He'd cursed them by denying what he was—what he *is*.

She picked up the second chair by the back and smashed it into the desk until it shattered in her hands.

A wolf.

She threw the remains away and moved toward the desk. She flipped it with a single swing. It crashed onto the last of the chairs. His chair.

A wolf.

She stomped at the desk until it splintered under her foot.

A wolf. The whole damn time.

She spun back on the room. Her whole body flexed as she screamed her throat raw. Doors ripped from the armoire, splintered chairs, broken drawer. It looked like the destruction following the first exodus, an event he had caused, along with every other that had brought her, brought them all, to the point of hate and open violence. She focused on the crushed folder on the floor. He had been a wolf the entire time.

"And he that curseth his father, or his mother . . . " she said.

She dropped to her knees. Every heavy breath rumbled out of her. Like it did from Zarker. Like it did from the creatures Virgil had convinced her to fight. Had conditioned her to believe were evil and vicious and damned. Creatures like him. Because that's what he'd wanted.

She stared at nothing in front of her. Adrenaline shook her from the inside out.

He wanted to die. He wanted punishment. Everything that had happened was because he was too much of a coward to admit what he was.

" . . . shall surely be put to death."

CHAPTER 9

NOT ONLY HAD MR. CRAWFORD KEPT RILEY'S room despite her disappearing, without paying rent for three months, he'd even cleaned the room in her absence, as though he believed that making the place nicer would cause her to come back from wherever she had disappeared to.

At another time Riley would've appreciated her landlord's kindness: the washed and stored dishes, the neatly hung bathroom towels, her clothes folded and tucked into the closet, the made bed. He'd even kept the spare key in the fake rock outside the door instead of changing the lock or renting the room to another person. She would have apologized, offered an explanation, promised to make up the lost rent, and thanked Mr. Crawford for his unwarranted patience. But that time, like many others, was gone.

Riley watched the sole of her right shoe flap as she kicked it onto the floor. She ripped the damp socks off and stuffed the pair of them into the left shoe, with a smaller hole in the toe. She yanked the gym bag out from the closet and unzipped the side pocket with such force it nearly broke off the slider. She paused to concentrate on any sounds coming from the other side of the house before removing the small picture from the side pocket. Her mother smiled from her place on the couch of the apartment neither of them would ever see again, at least not the way it looked then. Pointed lines formed in her cheeks from the smile, a mixture of wide-set features and age. Riley was there, too, although the look she gave indicated she preferred not to be. She remembered that day, finishing up the roll of Polaroid film she and he had purchased the previous weekend. Her mother insisted on the picture. "Is this how you want to be remembered?" she had asked after the image became clear. Riley had shrugged. "All right. How about one of you two?"

Riley couldn't help wondering how many more lines there now were on her mother's face. Had she started to let the gray show as a symbol of all she'd been forced to endure? A life of carrying secrets, her husband dying through the machinations of his own followers, raising her daughter alone, and then, finally, losing that daughter to the same sect her husband had led and died for. How many of those gray hairs and wrinkles had Riley caused?

She put the photo aside on the floor as she dug through the rest of the bag, tossing out the clothes Mr. Crawford had so neatly folded into the overstuffed compartment. She threw them out as though they were nothing, until reaching the very bottom of the bag. She tugged the old army jacket free. She clutched it in both hands in front of her as though praying to it. It felt like it had been a lifetime since she'd worn it, and yet another lifetime spent wearing it.

She hastily removed the tattered old coat Samantha had given her before they'd been forced from another apartment she'd likely never see again, after both of them had been deprived of places they called home. She looked over the cuff straps digging into the skin of her inner arm. The belt with its empty holster sagged on her hips, a sweat-stained T-shirt hanging over it. She surveyed the clothes strewn over the floor around her, stripping off the jeans and shirt she'd worn almost every day since the last time she'd stood in this room. She replaced them with a pair of black leggings and a black long-sleeved shirt she'd frequently worn during practice, both before and after her accident—not that it was an accident after all. It was nice not to have the blade's straps digging directly into her arm, and she adjusted the pistol until it sat less awkwardly on the back of her hip. They weren't the warmest clothes she had, but she could deal with the cold. She needed to be flexible, mobile. She needed to be the things that Virgil wasn't.

A fresh pair of socks felt like warm pillows over her feet. She wiggled her toes for a moment just to have the fabric flutter over them. She took a moment to admire the stitching along the edges of the one pair of sneakers she'd brought with her to Crawford's place. The solid threads, the nicely grooved interior. They were like finding a hundred dollars tucked into the rear pocket of a pair of forgotten jeans. Amazing how something as small as a good, reliable pair of shoes changed so much. As though she were human again.

The musty old smell struck her immediately as she pulled her father's army jacket over her arms. The smell was probably imaginary, but it seemed real to her. She threw her arms across her face and buried her nose in the crooks of her elbows. She breathed in deeply. Samantha had done the same to the clothing pile in her son's room. He was probably more present to her than Riley's father was now. Still, it was nice. It made her feel less alone. She looked at the photograph once again. Maybe she should have taken the other photo, the one with him, the way he had been before, the way *they* had been. The test was to retrieve something that reminded her of "who she is and why she chose to fight with us." *Us* meaning the Pointed Hand. *With* meaning alongside. She didn't think about it at the time but *with* could also mean against. She tucked the photo into the chest pocket under the badge reading McKNIGHT. She smoothed it against her. The last thing she had of her mother contained within the last thing she had of her father.

She buttoned the jacket up and pulled at the bottom. It was still quite big on her, long enough to cover the pistol on her side, but not nearly as large as she remembered it being, and nowhere near the bulk of the cloak she'd been trained in. The sleeves themselves were just wide enough to slip over the cuff on her arm and allow the blade to extend and retract, as though fitted for that purpose. She pulled at the ends of the jacket as she stood, pushed onto her toes, and leaned into her heels. She shook out her arms and legs, bouncing as she did so. She hadn't only become human again. She'd become more of herself than ever. What she was meant to be.

One more look over the room, her discarded clothes and old shoes lying among those she'd tossed out of the gym bag in the closet. Maybe Mr. Crawford would walk in to find this stuff and think she was back or maybe he'd think someone had broken in.

A lighter hue leaked under the door with locks on either side. There was still no sound behind it. It wouldn't take long to write a note at least, thank him for taking her in, allowing her to use his space and even watching the stuff that she had left behind. She remembered the black-and-white pictures on his living room wall of him, his wife, and the little girl hugging his wife's leg. In another photo the girl sat by herself on the trio of stairs at the front of the house, stretching her arms and legs out in snow, smiling so big that her eyes closed while wearing a helmet and posing next to an oversized bicycle. She was always in black and white. She was always a little girl. Color pictures continued of Crawford and his wife. Lines grew on their faces. Gray mixed into their hair. They had aged without her until, eventually, even his wife was gone. Maybe that was why he'd kept Riley's possessions safe and her room available. He hoped at least one person would come back.

Riley's eyes closed as she stood in front of the door that divided her life from that of the old man who'd allowed her to share his space where they could both live alone. Her father. His daughter. Her mother. His wife. Her best friend. Even her first "real" boyfriend. Who knows how many of his friends. At his age, he couldn't have been the last of everyone he'd known at her age.

She had paid for the room, but not for his kindness, his shelf of useful things, his offers of food and the loan of his car, his stewardship of her meager possessions in her absence. He'd guarded them, and all she did was storm in, make a mess, and leave. She was always going to leave because she knew exactly what would happen if she stayed. Death would come. Death in the form of Virgil or Dove or some other disguised figure. If they could find a way to attack her when surrounded by thirty-foot-high metal walls, they could find a way to attack her here. And they didn't care who was in their way. Not even someone she barely knew, a teacher she had barely spoken to in three years. Better not to know her. She took a deep breath as she opened her eyes again. Better he lived by himself than die because of her.

She didn't need to turn the lights off on her way out. She closed the door for the last time, locked it, and placed the key back under the fake rock. The fence on the side of the house required a couple of quick steps and an easy jump to get over. She stuck the landing through the thin layer of lonely snowflakes. She breathed steam into the crisp night. A light smell of moisture and trees lingered in the air.

There was a loud bark.

CHAPTER 10

A LONG STRING OF DOG BARKS ERUPTED FROM down the street at the very extent of her hearing, rapid as machine gun fire. Barks gave way to growls and yelps, then the shattering of glass and a sustained scream. Riley took off toward the noise.

Wind blew past her ears. Drifting snow scattered around her head. She wasn't sprinting into the tempest. She was the storm, bringing all the fury she carried with her.

Houses lit up as the sounds became louder. The barks spaced out with fewer variations in their sound until only one dog still cried out in a frightened, rhythmic alarm. The screams became constant, irregular, and overlapping as she charged down the block. Headlights of a stopped vehicle occupied the center of the narrow road ahead. The driver twisted to look back to where the sounds were coming from. Riley planted one foot on the front bumper. She leapt over the car's long roof, bounced off the flat trunk, and landed. She didn't lose a step.

The neighborhood buzzed with the activity of lights flipping on; residents peeking through windows and leaning out of doors; shouts, whispers, and phones lighting up. Two massive figures dashed across the road, bounding on hands and feet. These weren't the wolves she knew. These were feral, savage. Monsters. Murderers. Zarkers. The one in the front smashed through the railing of an elevated patio and through the half-opened front door of the house on her right. It was a quarter of a block away, still a few seconds before she could get there.

A gunshot and shriek tore through the house as the second beast leapt up the stairs.

Riley glanced to the other house as they drew closer. One dog still barked from the darkened interior. Short breaths punctuated the screams coming from the second floor. It was too far away for now.

She cut across the front lawn on her right. The second wolf turned as she sprang from the ground and over the railing. She ran along the front of the house. The wolf's eyes landed on her. Her fist landed between the wolf's eyes. Her left hand ached from the impact, but for now, the blade would remain sheathed.

The other wolf twisted toward her. A dark gray stripe forked over its back. It held a man by the shirt in front of itself. Blood poured from open wounds on the man's neck and across his chest. The blood on his throat bubbled with each breath. A pistol lay several feet from his reach, tossed closer to where a small child hid under a long table. The wolf growled through fangs thick with dripping blood. It released the man to dart toward her. She connected a sweeping kick to the wolf's snout. It hit the ground with a heavy thump while she touched the floor with barely a sound. Her eyes met those of the little boy under the table. Another scream ripped from the house across the road before the booming blast of a shotgun round.

"Run," she said before turning away from the boy.

She landed a quick elbow against the skull of the wolf starting to rise just outside the doorway. She ran straight off the top of the stairs and onto the road. Her knees immediately adjusted to the shock. The front window was shattered on the house facing her. Plates of jagged glass still clung to the frame. She shielded her face as she jumped through.

Glass sparkled up from the wooden floor. Blood streaked down the wall to the mound of a small dog, one leg kicking in a spasm. A second dog stained a patch of carpet behind the door. One string of flesh connected its head to its neck. Books were tossed near a pool of water, along with shiny blue pebbles from a shattered glass fish tank with blue and yellow fish flopping uselessly. Footsteps thumped against the ceiling above her, followed by rumbled breaths and hoarse screams. Pictures lined the wall in front of a staircase leading up and away from the front window. She lunged up the stairs, hitting only every fourth step, slowing as she turned at the landing between staircases.

She peeked through the railing, leaning to see around a cushioned seat and a coffee table. One gray wolf squatted in the far end of the room. A woman pulled herself into a ball in the corner, pushing her head back as though trying to melt into the wall. The wolf stared at her, both of its claws planted on the floor between them. A few small scratches barely bled on her shoulder. It watched her taking quick but quiet breaths, remaining still almost as though guarding her. Possibly even pitying her.

"Humans," rumbled a voice from the room

behind the wall the woman wanted to push through. "Comfortable too long."

Riley took one careful step forward. She placed one finger over her lips as the woman's eyes caught hers. The crouched wolf tilted its head. She took another step. The wolf sniffed the air. It turned. She smashed her fist against the top of its snout. The wolf's jaw smacked the floor, and he recoiled back up. She landed a punch solid against its eye socket. It dropped to the floor beneath a large window.

"Never had to live in fear."

The woman's eyes were wide staring up at Riley. She drew in a deep breath. Riley shushed her once more.

"Never learned—" The words stopped. Riley stepped back from the woman in the corner and away from the wolf knocked out on the floor.

A growl rumbled through the doorway like an avalanche. Inside, a lamp was shattered under an overturned mattress. Blood drops on the carpet led around and out of her sight. One wolf leaned to peek out through the doorway. It stared at her curiously. Riley locked her jaw and stared into its eyes. It took a step back as a growl rose from inside the room. Hollow footsteps shook the floor. A massive figure, outlined by spiked tufts, stepped into view.

His bright red eyes burned like lava. Long claws molded over his wide fingers, sharp as glass, thick as stone. Dirt, grime, and old blood caked into the spiked fur covering his arms and shoulders. He rumbled like an oncoming train. His lip curled into a demented smile.

Riley took a short step back.

Zarker turned to fit through the doorway. He looked down at the wolf on the floor. A small crack of blood trickled over the bridge of its nose. The woman pushed herself against the corner, quaking in fear. He glanced over his shoulder to the second wolf who seemed to watch in odd fascination. He turned his attention back to Riley, eyes locking, laser sights on a target.

Riley released her blade.

He growled. “Mine.”

“Not this time,” Riley growled back.

Zarker roared. A torrent of spit flew from his maw.

Riley braced herself, staggering her stance and rolling onto the balls of her feet. She placed one hand back to gauge the room behind her while the other hand remained forward, blade ready to thrust. Zarker blocked out the entire doorway behind him. A short hallway led to two other doors, one open and one closed, and ended at a smaller window. Zarker stalked forward, cutting off Riley's lane into the hall. She shuffled toward the stairs. Last time, in front of the fountain, there'd been more room to dodge and maneuver. Yet he still caught up to her. She needed to be more careful with her distance. Controlled. Precise. She needed to be his opposite.

Zarker lunged forward. Riley jumped back. He spun into the narrow gap in front of the stairs. She leapt over them and vaulted off the banister on the other side. He followed over the gap, smashing through the railing as she backed toward the hallway. He continued his charge. She jumped, kicking off the wall and over him. His impact knocked a large dent into the wall. She rolled over the floor and bounced onto the coffee table next to the staircase. Spit streaked as he turned toward her again, crouched on the round tabletop. He bared his teeth at her, growling, yet not charging again.

"Kill you," he snarled, "rip you apart."

"Heard that one before," she replied.

She dodged just as he smashed the table with one tree-trunk arm. Riley swung around him. She looped one hand over his shoulder to pull herself up. She plunged the blade into the mound of muscle between his neck and shoulder. She kicked off him, back flipping away before he could swipe his heavy arms at her. She landed in the middle of the floor.

"Oh God. Oh God. Oh God," the woman panted as she rocked in the corner, eyes huge in terror darting between Riley, Zarker, and the gray wolf still out on the floor nearby.

"Tear the flesh from your bones," he growled.

"Catch me first," Riley answered, shuffling toward the corner away from the woman and the wolf.

Zarker roared as he stretched back to grab the arm of the chair behind him. He flung it toward Riley. She rolled away as the chair smashed into one wall and ricocheted into the other. She continued to roll as Zarker slammed one claw into the floor. The woman in the corner screamed. His arm tensed as he pulled his razor-tipped fingers from the floor, shooting particles and torn fabric and wood dust into the air around it. Riley swept around to land a sharp kick to the side of Zarker's knee. She felt a bone crack in her foot. The massive wolf barely moved.

"Oh God. Oh God. Oh God," the woman repeated in the corner as an unfinished prayer.

Zarker craned his long neck around to follow Riley as she backpedaled over the pieces of the shattered banister. Her foot stung with every other step. His red eyes watched her from over his shoulder, the black centers were needle tips among the burning color. The spot of blood on his shoulder mixed into the roots of one pointed clump of hair. His breaths were growls.

"Oh God. Oh God. Oh God."

"Quiet!" Zarker roared, turning to the woman in the corner. His head continued to turn as though looking over the wolf on the floor. He stared back at Riley. She remained next to the broken railing in the passage between the stairs and a set of tall bookshelves lining the wall. They stared at each other a moment. In the silence, Riley could hear the short, rapid breaths of another person inside the bedroom across from her, and the heavy, rumbling ones of the wolf who remained in that room. Riley locked into the dark center of Zarker's blazing red eyes.

"Think you're the strongest," she said, raising one hand and waving her fingers back and forth at him, "then come get me."

His lips peeled back to the dark red gums holding

in two lines of impossibly large teeth. The two fangs at the top nearly crossed the two at the bottom.

"Come on," she said again. "Try and catch me."

He started to turn toward her.

"Oh God. Oh God."

"Quiet," he said, spinning back, his arm swinging into a backhand strike.

"Don't." Riley started as she sprang forward, cutting across the gap in the floor. She leapfrogged over the remaining railing and over the broken table just as the arm swept forward. She jumped at Zarker's back as a hard blow knocked the woman's head against the corner. Riley buried her blade in Zarker's upper back as blood splattered on the wall. Riley gripped a handful of Zarker's caked hair. She ripped the blade out of him. She screamed as she plunged it back in. Zarker reached one massive arm over his back. A vice grip closed around Riley's shoulder. Another clamped onto the back of her neck.

Zarker spun as he locked onto Riley, still positioned on his back. He squeezed until the tips of his nails scratched and pierced into the skin along the sides of her neck, digging deeper as she tried to wiggle free. He staggered back before throwing himself against the wall. She heard the crack from impact. He held on to slam her into the wall one more time.

His grip loosened. Riley slid off and crashed onto the floor, seated against the base of the wall. She clutched at her chest. Her shallow breaths throbbed with pain. They brought no air into her lungs, as though she'd been flattened. She heard herself struggle for air. Her blade arm flailed uselessly at her side and her legs twitched in front of her. She saw the world jostling in front of her as she rocked back and forth. It was so clear—no shadows, colors she couldn't name, clearer than any other person could ever see it—yet distant. She couldn't speak, move, feel. Frozen, both her and the world around her.

The woman in the corner slumped against the wall, like Riley did, blood pouring from a large gash on the side of her face. Her chest rose and fell, unlike Riley's. The wolf had begun to stir from the floor. The crack on its nose healed, the blood dried. It blinked until the faded red darkened. Her eyes rose as she finally drew in one breath, a searing pain following the air as her chest expanded at last. Zarker stared down at her. He hunched over like a predator mocking its prey.

"Caught you," he said.

His hand slammed into her, pinning her against the base of the wall. One hand covered her entire right chest and shoulder. He dug his fingers in to pin the arm at her side. He pulled his face to hers. Heavy, acrid breath stung her nose. She could nearly taste the dirt, grease, and grime that clumped the ends of his hair together. She felt the heat of his eyes burn into the back of her skull. His long fangs were yellowed, the tips barely sharp enough to pierce. He wrapped his other hand completely over her left arm.

"You take our blood," she heard as though whispered directly into her brain. "I take it back."

She felt his grip tighten over her. He pulled her forward. He swung his head back and thrust it toward her. His jaws clamped over her other shoulder, the force of his bite stabbed dulled teeth through her flesh. She screamed. He shook his head, teeth shredding through her skin. A growl ripped through him and into her. Satisfaction.

She was lifted from the floor. Her weight pulled down, tearing more of the flesh around the teeth and nails dug over both of her shoulders and onto her back. She kicked weakly, the tips of her shoes barely brushing the thick hair over his chest. He gave one more shake before releasing his jaws. The air stung the wounds encircling her entire shoulder. She screamed in pain.

She tried to swing as he suspended her there, upper arms pinned to her sides, forearms swinging as useless little stumps, legs kicking at nothing but air. Her blade barely scratched at his elbow.

His curled lip twitched as he held her in front of him. He licked the blood from his front teeth. His hair over his throat waved as the muscle beneath rippled from swallowing.

"We fear you too long," he said. "We were always stronger. Time for you to fear." He shook her. Her legs swung like a ragdoll. "No," he said, shaking his long face at her. "You don't live in fear." He licked his chops once more. "You die in it."

The grip on her left arm released. Then darkness came. His hand covered her entire face, a small gap between his thumb and forefinger.

"Fear," he said again. "The last thing you'll ever know."

Riley felt herself being lifted higher from the floor. She flew backward. She heard a loud crack and saw a burst of lights as her head slammed against the wall. Her mouth gaped open under his hand. She flew forward, her arms and legs swinging limply, and back once more. There was no crack. There were no stars. He was a blur of muddy colors and shadows. Darkness followed.

She watched the world fade.